I0748400

LIMERICKS OF LOSS AND REGRET

MARTY BARRETT

FOGELFOOT press

LIMERICKS OF LOSS AND REGRET

First Printing, 2020

ACKNOWLEDGMENTS

To Donald Bailey, late Lowell High School classical languages teacher, whose puns and blazers were as loud as his Latin was precise. To Edward Gorey and Rob Halford, who were never photographed together. To the multiple people who showed me kindness during my Personal Plague Times that preceded Everyone's Plague Times. To my children, Marisol and Harrison, who are all whimsy, darkness, and kindness in bright-eyed skeletal wraith-bairn form. To Richard Brautigan, Dead Brad Moore, the extant Todd Bearson, Derek Dexheimer, Shawna Shilmover, John Underkoffler, and Ghost Gordon Thunderfoot—they know what they did.

Preface to the Second Edition

• Did you know that groupies of 70s yacht-rocker Boz Scaggs are *themselves* known as Boz Scaggs? **You see?**

• Did you know that, following German reunification, the *Duden Wörterbücher* approved the word *Abdeckbandnamenkonvention* to describe a process by which one would choose a name for their tribute band? Thus the Bloody Well Righteous Brothers: The Supertramp Experience Featuring Horst und Matti Dammerung, appearing nightly at the Flughaven Frankfurt Holiday Inn. Note: the Dammerungs' *Abdeckbandnamenkonvention* might not have been the *Abdeckbandnamenkonvention* employed by We're A German Band, Munich's resident Grand Funk Railroad outfit, fronted by former hotel detective Ulli Splatter. **Do you *see*?**

• I was commissioned to design a modern cemetery—the kind where the husks of our departed can be tapped to power those "Beware of Migrants" signs. I brought in a Powerpoint presentation with a lot of John Tesh in it. "We were hoping for a diorama," the funders said. "All cemeteries are die-o-ramas," I said, and swept out (I was wearing an opera cape). **Do you see?** (Angels are real.)

—Between the magma and the Chandler Bike Path, February, 2025

This Page Intentionally Left Frank.

I'm sorry, Frank, but I have to do what's right for me. I've taken your bus pass and a box of empties. If you must know, I'm meeting a man from the motor trade. I don't care what you think about these fingernails. They're SEXY. Clack! Clack! Clack! I'm Count Orlok. Your dog might as well be a cat.

I'm speaking My Truth. I took a quiz about which Kirkland Signature item I was and after a few tries I got the Tilapia package that I felt I deserved. You don't know me.

A WORD

This book contains 50 limericks and 50 short stories, or thereabout. For this second, International Cormorant edition, there is also what we in the trade call "value-added content," with the emphasis on the Ent, as Treebeard's wife used to say.

The limericks are titled, which is revolutionary.

It is the author's fervent hope that you recognize what a special time you live in.

"NO ONE TALKS, SINGS, OR CREATES filmed entertainment about 18-wheelers anymore," she said. The waves looked phosphorescent through the heavy, floor-to-ceiling windows. Despite her great ennui, she was happy to be rich. "And I think we can agree that Tokyo is a better contender to be called 'Shakytown' than Los Angeles.

"Is there some international standards body we can appeal to, or do we just have to, you know, take it?" She placed her fingertips tentatively on the glass. "I don't know CBs."

She thought: *"I was raised here in this living hell."*

Alan approached softly, wearing a turtleneck and flowing linen pants, the stems of two massive snifters separated by a doughy finger, slightly swollen by hypertension medication, in his right hand. He never knew how to respond when she got like this. Sometimes he felt like she was a bat, shrieking and echolocating off the walls, which was him. And if these walls could talk, she would tell them that talking was above their pay grade. So just shut up and exist so that I know where I am.

"How does Steely Dan fit in?" he asked. It's true that Steely Dan was never far from his mind, even if Peg (that was her name, the name of his favorite Steely Dan song, the specialty by which he found her in the back of an alternative weekly, and what his dog had for a rear left leg) grew weary of hearing about "The Dan," and delighted in sporting her David Palmer-branded swimsuit at their Bogue Chitto Marina timeshare.

"Well they just fucking *don't*," Peg said.

—for Ben Deily and Great White Sharks in love everywhere

CONTENTS

CHAPTER I

WHAT HAS BECOME OF YOU?

I broke several lobes in a fall
And now cannot function at all
So each day I sit
In warm, ropy spit
And listen to Pink Floyd's "The Wall."

CHAPTER II

CORMORANT

IT WAS GOLDEN HOUR for Angie. Just after sunup, even the crumbs on the Formica surface cast shadows, and a jelly smudge was a purple glacier, as if the corpse of Grimace Himself had been found, thawed and tumbled out of a snowbank, to make for McDonaldland an April filled with grief. She leaned into the tabletop and scraped off some crusted grilled cheese, then gave both her manicure and the booth a swipe with a damp rag. This had been Carla's table last night, but some people couldn't be bothered.

She was 20 minutes into a double shift; the sun was telegraphing through the passing trucks, shining on the swamps, the Parkway, the lot, and directly in her face. She imagined the view wasn't pleasant, her lipstick garish and extra-dimensional to the customers who happened to look, whether they were travelers all jazzed up for diner food or the regulars who returned out of inertia. But Vito was waiting at home, and he loved her no matter what shape her nails were in, who was right in the last fight, or the mileage between when they'd met and now. Still, she wanted a cigarette.

"How you holding up?" said Frank, eggy fork in hand, hefting a sturdy cup of coffee. He was a regular, hauling oranges up to New Hampshire and Maine.

Angie arranged herself with one hand on a cocked hip, knowing its effect on someone like Frank, while she watched the sun catch the steam from his mug.

"I want a cigarette," she said.

"You quit again," he said.

"Just before work," she said.

She supposed it was a kind of freedom no longer pretending she liked her job, or that she had anywhere else to go. Freedom from the compulsion to invent something.

She remembered that period after her father left and her mother was getting the ducks aligned. Angie would round the corner from the TV room to the kitchen to find her mother with head bent over the want ads, forearm perpendicular to the table, cigarette between two fingers, coffee at elbow, the smoke and steam curling together in the morning sun. Peaceful. Angie would back out and let her mother have this time. She suspected Adele would lure a man before she landed a job, and the first of two stepfathers rolled in quickly.

If it had been up to Angie, her mother would have found a job instead, and the two of them would have smoked at that kitchen table together. She was 15 back then, her mother 41. They could have made it work. They didn't need anyone else.

But first came stepdad Arthur, and then, when her mother was 46, Bob. If there had ever been a window to make it an exclusive mother/daughter thing, Angie had missed it.

When Bob left, Adele quit smoking and sold the house. Angie met Vito at the mill, and they moved in together. Her mother had never liked Vito—had, in fact, gloated when he'd had his injury—but at least Vito wasn't going anywhere.

She squinted at the sunrise, focusing at a speck out on the swamps. It felt like the coffee was kicking in. Her mood brightened.

"Can you kick a couple of those oranges off the back?" she asked Frank.

On an inland islet, the cormorant pointed its head toward the morning traffic and the diner beyond it. An eel lay drying in his beak. The cormorant gobbled the eel and looked around to see if it had dropped any eel orts. No, nothing to speak of. Did the diner have eels? Better not risk it. The cormorant may or may not have been considering the solid, vibrant relationship of Angie and Vito.

A couple of exits from where the cormorant and Angie regarded each other, it had been a rough morning in the double-wide. Vito woke to pain, his prescriptions used up. Angie rubbed salve on his leg. He was ashamed, cranky. He didn't want to need her help.

"Let me take care of this," she said. He fell back on the pillow and sighed.

"I'm an invalid," he said.

"Just until you get on your feet," she said.

*****

Vito didn't know how the elderly did it, holding each other up, going to doctors' appointments, wiping each other's faces, knowing the menu. His own sisters might smile at an old couple like that, but not him. They took the long view, maybe, but all he saw was acceptance, the inevitability of death, making the best of a bad situation. Reduced Circumstances and Hopelessness. He would never walk without a significant limp, and it pissed him off. The outside of his knee looked apocalyptic and the inside was made of bank-breaking Outer Space technology.

"I'll do the rest myself," he said, trying not to sound unkind. He didn't want to think of Angie as a nurse. It was sexy when she cooked for him, when she helped him shovel snow, or when she beat him in video games; not when she was tossing out his rank dressings.

"Call me if you need something," she said, her joints cracking as she stood. "I'll see you in 17 hours."

He reached for her, hoping to bring her full, pleasant weight down on him, even if it would be painful. But she had to work.

Instead she leaned back down and cupped him, through his sweatpants, with her small hand. It wasn't pity.

"I love you," she said.

"I love you," he said.

He watched her leave, listened as she took care to keep the door from snapping back, as she crossed the lot to the highway, where her manager would pick her up at the entrance to the trailer park.

Keeping his leg still, he wiggled his toes. There they stood like a firing squad way down there. Then he gingerly moved his leg from the bed, and clenched his teeth through the pain. He sat up, sweating.

Two months before he had tried to kick his hat out of the smelter when the foreman's son, visiting for the afternoon, had backed into the vice. He had just managed to edge the kid away when the iron contraption slammed shut. His kneecap fell apart like a sandcastle. Vito had never felt pain like that, and his first instinct was to punch the boy. He couldn't even do that. He passed out briefly, pitching backward. He saw the kid peering from behind the foreman's window as the stretcher carried him out, probably restricted to iPad games for the rest of the shift.

Angie got the afternoon off and sat with him in the tiny room he shared with two other patients. She smiled grimly when the shop steward walked in.

"I don't get why your hat was in the smelter," Dave Ciriello said.

"The point is I wasn't smelted," Vito argued, propped up, trying to keep his voice down. "Jimmy bumped into the vice. If he hadn't been there - "

" - if you hadn't had your leg in the vice, this would not have happened," Dave said. "We can't fight it as a workplace safety issue. You're supposed to be 18 inches away from that thing anyway. The camera has you goofing around for 30 seconds before the kid even shows up."

The best the union could do was keep his job available for three more months. Dave, who happened to have dated Angie for about two minutes in high school, wasn't about to go out on a limb.

"We can probably get you on in Shipping," Dave said, knowing what the answer would be.

Vito turned his face away. Dave grew uncomfortable and left.

"All I want to do is smelt," Vito said.

In the dark trailer Vito felt sorry for himself. Sounds of highway traffic filtered through the park. He listened as he steeled himself to stand. Beyond the traffic, deep in the swamp islets, he could almost hear the cormorant. The noise it made, kind of a strangled <cack!>, was reassuring, somehow, in its existence.

With a grunt, Vito rose to make himself some coffee.

*****

It was 9:15 p.m. and Carla was just breezing in. Oh, fuck her, thought Angie.

Carla was 19 and she liked it. Angie had once watched as Carla dumped a half-gallon of iced tea in the lap of Angie's landlord, who then tipped her. Meanwhile, Angie had forgotten Mr. Hanraghan's cheesecake a week before and she worried she was going to get evicted.

Carla stood at the counter, hand on cocked hip, trying it out, making eyes at her boyfriend revving his engine in the parking lot.

"Carla," Angie said. "Let's fucking go."

"Sorry," Carla said, moving her fat ass just barely. Angie had met Carla's mother in the laundry room of the trailer park. They were both 34.

Carla clocked in and spun around like she was in "Chicago."

"Allright," she said to the diner full of middle-aged men. "Which one of you dirty old bastards wants a refill?"

Angie pushed open the door to the parking lot to a chorus of "Me! Me!" The $60 she'd made in tips that day, and whatever she made tomorrow, was going straight to the electric bill, but at least Juancho in the kitchen had set her up with a bag of dinner to eat with Vito in front of the TV. She reached for her keys, then remembered she hadn't driven today. Securing a ride home had completely slipped her mind.

"Fuck!" she said.

"Let's at least have a cigarette first," Frank said.

"Jesus," Angie said, watching Frank emerge, not at all wholesomely, from the shadows.

"Didn't see your car here," he said. "You need a ride?"

"Yeah, I'll take a cigarette, too," Angie said. "Fuck it."

On its inland islet, the cormorant spread its wings, then reclined, such as it could. It might be inferred from its stance that it was considering the tumult of Angie's mind at that moment, or simply that it had dimly registered the appearance of a styrofoam take-out container that had spent the day blowing toward him from the Parkway.

They stamped out their butts, with Angie vowing she'd quit again tomorrow. They walked to Frank's car, a Key Lime eyesore at the edge of the lot.

In the low-slung passenger pilot seat of Frank's Camaro, Angie smelled some combination of stripper body spray and bags of truck stop jerky. She could see evidence of one collecting at her feet, but was happy to see no remnants of the other.

"Vinnie still laid up?" Frank said.

"It's Vito," Angie replied, "and Yes, but he's getting stronger every day."

"Is he gonna be gimpy for the long term?" asked Frank, "walker with tennis balls?"

"That's not Vito," Angie said, just imagining it, and smiling. "He says he'll kill himself if he - "

"You need a man with all four limbs," Frank said, peeling out onto the highway. "Hot thing like you."

Frank was already traveling at a pretty good clip. She couldn't very well have told him to stop, nor could she jump out without injury and loss of dinner. Maybe she would have done that at Carla's age, but two cripples without jobs wasn't an option now, so she shut up.

"Am I right?" Frank said loudly, and she stiffened. She realized he had been drinking. The cigarettes had masked the smell in the parking lot, but in the confines of his car it smelled like a yeast infection. The park was two exits down, and they traveled the rest of the way in silence, almost.

"I'm just saying," he said, but she didn't answer. They soon arrived at the entrance.

She thought she could make a clean break, said "Thank you!" a little too brightly, pushed at the door, but Frank already had two handfuls of her.

At this moment Vito shambled out of the trailer, his first time outside all day. It was nearly ten, and he was hoping Angie hadn't elected to pull a triple (she had done this at least twice before, and AJ would throw in an extra $50 out of kindness) but, if she had, why hadn't she called?

He saw the green monstrosity idling at the gate an eighth of a mile away, and knew Angie was in there. He'd seen that car—who could have missed it?—at the diner before.

"I'll kick your fucking teeth in," Angie said, swinging her doggie bag in the limited space, connecting with Frank's cheek. The bag's contents spattered everywhere, on the two of them, and all over the dashboard, which looked like an airplane console, glowing with pretty or douchey lights, depending on whether they were in a nursery or a Camaro. She decided they were douchey.

"Fuck," Frank said, doubling down. He grabbed at her skirt again and actually tore part of it. This time Angie elbowed him in the face, bloodying his nose, and got out of the car.

"Don't come to the diner again," she said, "or I'll cut your goddamn head off."

The Camaro roared away, its still-open door narrowly missing Angie, who stood there brushing rice off herself. At the gate appeared Vito, his crutches wobbling, his face slick. He took one good look at her, then told himself a story.

"You threw me under the bus," he said.

*****

From his inland islet, the cormorant took wing, quickly rising high enough to spy Atlantic City, the Pine Barrens, New York, Philadelphia, and Montreal. A pod of whales signaled from the Arctic Circle, dim through the ancient fogs that allow all animals to communicate with each other. But that isn't what the cormorant was looking for. What I'm telling you is that no one knows what he was looking for.

Angie, her lipstick smeared, her dress torn, feeling betrayed by something she couldn't name, faced her husband on the soft shoulder.

"Vito!" Angie cried, "it is you that I do love!" and sobbed. He just looked at her.

It was just too much. She had no idea if he would work again, every paycheck was spent before she got it, her job gave her very little pleasure, and coming home was like entering a tomb. Now she had this shit to deal with. He had better not give her one more ounce of this misery.

Vito's eyes stung, and he looked at the moon. Something flying up there. For a moment he forgot where he was, and he was a child again, traveling with his parents to Dover, leaving Jersey for some reason. He remembered his father piloting this boat of a Buick over the swamps, Scull Bay, Shelter Island Bay, Lakes Bay. Turning to his mother in the front seat, Vito Sr. had said, "Why would anyone want to leave New Jersey?" To this day Vito didn't know, either. Although he might give Vegas a try, he thought.

But Angie stood before him in the moonlight. Her chest was heaving. She looked like she'd been in a fight. She was covered in rice. Her sobs subsiding, she made a noise like <cack!> and Vito hobbled over to her. He dropped his crutches and held her.

"You've got half as much underneath, but we've got twice as much above," she said.

She abandoned her plastic bag of leftovers and they helped each other to the trailer, where they lay together, their foreheads touching, exhausted.

The cormorant alighted on the side of the road and ate both the rice and the pork chop, leaving the salad.

CHAPTER III

THAT'S WHAT IT WAS TO BE ALIVE

Said Emily Webb, lying dead
"To think of the worms that I've fed!
If it all ends the same
—Grover's Corners or Maine—
I'd have moved to Billerica instead."

CHAPTER IV

INNISFREE

RAY DIDN'T KNOW how she did it, but now Audrey was covered in bees. Yes it creeped him out, but there was something else. Why had *he* never inspired that kind of devotion? He wondered what it was like.

He remembered some of the old ladies he'd done odd jobs for back in Twisty River. Each wore sweatpants and smelled of Orally-Familiar Dog; several times Ray had appeared in one mudroom or another, red-faced from late autumn leaf raking, there for his five bucks, and he'd catch one of them really giving it to the dog in the mouth.

It was gross, but then you never saw the dogs complaining. And his employers were unashamed. It would have mortified young Ray had one of his elderly benefactors turned to him and said, "Why does this one happiness disgust you?"

Ray was sitting on the hill outside BlimpCorp, chasing some salad around a plastic container with a spork. He'd just cornered a piece of stray carrot when he saw her through the lid, like a TV show on a plane.

So there was Audrey, a bee-loud glade of one, flailing around in the middle of the street, being adored like both comb and queen. She was always someone's center of attention, and now it was these bees.

He'd once loved Audrey; had believed everything she'd said. But he was starting to associate love with betrayal, because one too often left the porch light on for the other. How do you move on from that? He scooped up the last carrot. Sometimes, when the only tool in your toolbox is a spork, everything begins to smell like fruit cocktail.

This was insane. He thought of all those delicious WMDs available in Iraq, Iran, whatever, and the fervor they inspired. Was the fervor not real because the WMDs didn't exist? Just because Audrey wasn't gonna happen didn't mean Ray should put his guns in the ground.

Those bees certainly seemed to love Audrey. Ray wanted to let her know it was all right by him.

"I don't understand, Audrey," Ray said to the distant figure, "and maybe I'll never understand, but I'm happy for you."

It was good to say this—good to mean it.

"I release you."

Audrey had been shopping at Macy's when she walked through another woman's cloud of just-sprayed perfume. Audrey's own frank secretions were all over the pH scale, which is why it was dangerous for her to ever wear a third-party scent. She'd always worn this very earthy fragrance called Pile, which doubled as shoe polish for miners.

But today she smelled different, and as she flounced past an old tree on her way to lunch, something about her excited the hive. By the time Ray saw her, she had been driven into the street and was calling for help, but her mouth was full of bees and no one understood her peril.

"We love what we love, Audrey," said Ray, tears in his eyes, and he turned and headed back to work.

Audrey ran onto the light rail track where the bee situation quickly became the least of her worries.

CHAPTER V

RESTROOM MANDATE

Lurking in lavat'ry stalls
My Congressman fondly recalls
His Patriot's Glee
At getting to see
    All those deportable balls.

CHAPTER VI

#BFST AT THE SECOND GUESS CAFE

HIS SERVER APPROACHED, and Ray was ready.

"Here's your cheese plate," she said. "You ordered it."

"I sure did," said Ray, determined—maybe uncharitably so—not to be taken in by the signature tactics of the trendy new restaurant so adored by neurodivergent influencers and the targeted ads that swirled around them.

"Look at Mr. Decisive," the manager said, pausing to stop in front of Ray's table. "Read somewhere that cheese isn't as bad as everybody thinks it is, did you?"

"Just because it isn't good for me doesn't mean I don't like it," Ray said, smiling.

The busboy, halfway through refreshing Ray's coffee, abruptly sat down at the table and, plopping his chin on his hands, asked dreamily:

"What is it like to know yourself so well?"

"You guys are great," Ray said, and for a few minutes no one talked to him.

It was a theme restaurant. Diners came to be talked down to by bitter college graduates, Bernie supporters, divorcees.

Ray activated a mid-size portable electronic device, placing it gently on the glass surface of the rickety table, and scrolled through celebrity gossip sites. At one point he had to gingerly napkin some Gruyere from the screen. Then the battery went dead because Ray had forgotten to charge it.

He put away the device and realized they were all looking at him.

"Was it worth it?" the waitress said.

"Yeah," said the busboy. "You enjoy your breakfast more when everybody gets to see you reading your little stories on your tablet?"

The staff began busily arranging the food. "Tweet a picture," they said. "Write 'nom nom nom' under it."

The manager smiled at him. "If this seems too chaotic to take a picture of your food, we have a little area over there where you can prop up the dish and light it the right way. Would you like that, or do you just want to eat your fucking meal?"

"No," Ray said, "my battery just died."

"Can I offer you a book now that you can't look at post-natal-baby-weight-loss bikini photos of Sassy McSassypants, star of NBC's 'The Shit'?" said the manager. "Or does holding paper make you nostalgic and you have to Snap your feels?"

"I'm fine just eating," murmured Ray.

"And we're all sure you are," said a delivery man with a sneer.

When he was through with his meal, he pushed the plate slightly away from himself to signal the waitress for the check.

"*Really*?" she said. "Is that what people do now?"

Rather than ask to break a twenty, Ray left a 30 percent tip. The manager glanced at the money on the table as Ray got up to leave.

"That's a nice tip for a 14-dollar check," he said. "Sure you want to do that, Big Spender?"

"Oh yes, yes," Ray said. "I love it here."

"That's so nice of you to say," the manager said, not looking at him. "You could write one of those extra-literary Yelp reviews that are so helpful to everyone."

"Yes! Yes!" Ray said, anxious to go.

"Really hope to see you soon," the manager said, walking away through most of saying it.

"I'll see you tomorrow!" Ray said, knowing that he couldn't let them win, and the next day the food was even worse.

CHAPTER VII

3-DAY BETRAYAL INTENSIVE

"Shift it, my guy, do not carry it,"
Says post-penitent Judas Iscariot.
"This weekend we'll tame
Your well-deserved shame
For 99 bucks at the Marriott."

CHAPTER VIII

CAVEAT EMPTOR

WHY SOMEONE WAS EXPECTING TO SELL A ROCK at a yard sale was one of those things that ultimately comforted Ray about humanity: he still didn't get most of it.

After determining it wasn't there to hold something down, Ray guessed that maybe the kid of the family was trying to help out with his own contribution and the parents were humoring him.

The rock had a satisfying shape and heft, though, the way a good baseball or gun feels, or a heavy tumbler of an afternoon libation. He brought the rock over to the sunhatted woman collecting cash on the lawn.

"Is this your son's contribution?" Ray asked. "You know, I kind of like it."

"Where did you get that?" the woman said, her eyes widening.

Ray didn't understand. He could see that something was wrong—the woman's husband, sensing a tone in his wife's voice audible only to him, had appeared from the house—so he thought he'd just AP Style Manual it.

"I found this rock by those books a minute ago," Ray said carefully, "and I wanted to see how much it was."

"You monster," the husband said. “Kevin!”

He was a small man, and much older than Ray, but it looked like he was about to take a swing at him. Should Ray take one for the team and absorb a punch from this guy?

"Whoa," Ray said. "I don't know what you're talking about. I just picked up this rock. Back off."

Ray was just laying the rock back on the books when he felt the old man thump him—hard—from behind. Ray crashed to the ground, the rock still in his hand.

"Not again! Not again!" the mom was screaming, as Ray blindly crawled out from under the man, then sprang to his feet and turned to face him.

"Get out of here, Bastard!" the man said. "Get out of here, you unblinking piece of shit!"

In that moment, Ray could think of nothing worse than paying the penalty for something he hadn't done. He wasn’t dumb. He knew that not every baseless accusation led to an adventure deep inside the forest with a friendly bear and visiting companions who didn’t stay too long—a reprieve only afforded to Grizzly Adams. What in the Sam Hill was happening? These people were his down-the-street neighbors, and he had walked by their home for years.

"The fuck out of here," the man said, puffing up. Ray could take him out with one punch, he thought. That would have to be enough. He walked home, holding the rock.

It wasn't until he sat down in his living room and placed the rock on the coffee table, drink in his hand, that Ray figured it out.

It wasn't a rock, it was a child's skull. And Ray was drunk.

"Oh Jeez!" Ray said. "It was probably their kid's *head*!"

CHAPTER IX

ME & JULIO LAMENT OUR SCHOOL'S LOW API SCORE

The candidate, dripping with wrath
Decreed in re: Common Core Math:
"No liberal blight
Can limit my right
To count all my parts in the bath."

CHAPTER X

WAY UP FIRM AND HIGH

IT SEEMED LIKE YESTERDAY, but it was oh, so long ago.

System Of A Down on Main Street, an earnest lesbian Bob Seger cover band, woke every morning through their German tour to a delicious and strengthening breakfast of coffee, fresh juice, turkey bacon, oatmeal with raisins in it, and a type of pastry they'd all fallen in love with in Dresden called *kleinflaff*, which was like a sweet pumpernickel bagel and which their tour manager, Debbie Margulis, had been thoughtful enough to have available throughout the trip.

It was eerie how each "soadomite" (there were six) could capture Bob Seger's spirit, voice, and phrasing. Each sported a bushy mane and, with the help of a competent backup band known as the Lycanthropes (1. because werewolves are killed by silver bullets and 2. because of the German fascination with supernatural weirdness, like the Scorpions) would take turns singing the big Seger hits. Then, at the end of the night, the six women would all return to the stage for a rousing showstopper of "Katmandu."

"Now that we're getting out of here–we'll see you in Katmandu! Good night!" The leader, Kendra Jorgensen, would yell, and they'd all bound from the stage to throaty Teuton screams.

"Katman*don't* do anything we wouldn't do!" added Janie Lewandowski, the youngest.

Thus the show traveled to steadily greater press and ticket sales throughout the just recently-united Deutschland. It was inevitable, though, that some party-pooping naysayer would ask in a press conference or radio interview how the band's sexual and political views could possibly be reconciled with their occupation, as a tribute act to a man who to no one's knowledge courted a lesbian fan base.

Molly-Anne Nobrega, the talkative one, would take this opportunity to make plain that there wasn't more of a progressive dyke out there than Bob Seger, whose "Down on Main Street" detailed a girl's first experimentation with female+female action and whose "Old Time Rock & Roll" was a paean to sexual diversity and thoughtful activism. "I can't listen to 'Like A Rock' on those Chevrolet commercials," she'd say, "without thinking about how supportive my mother was when I came out to her."

The group landed in Stuttgart to a fever pitch of positive publicity. "I'm living a dream," yelled Susan Rocco, whose specialty was "House (Behind the House)," a latter-day Seger smash, to clamorous fans outside the Rhine Center, "I feel like I'm standing as bright as the sun on that California coast."

"Which California coast?" her delighted fans yelled back dutifully.

"The *California coast* of being proud of who you *are*, comprising that *California beach* of *women helping each other,* and living in those *Hollywood Nights* of *not having to apologize for your orientation*!"

This exchange would repeat at tour stops all across the country, and the crowd just ate it up. MTV Europe played their "Against the Wind/ We've Got Tonite" medley with Roxette and Ace of Base over and over.

It was like a dream, a wonderful dream, but the dreamer had to awaken. After three sold-out nights in Berlin, the women of System Of A Down on Main Street headed back home to St. Augustine for a well-deserved rest. But then the group began to fall apart.

While cycling in Seneca Falls, Willow Abstrug met and later fell in love with a librarian from Atlanta and regretfully quit the band. Kendra herself, who'd been with the group since it was known as The Seger Beavers, decided to go back to school. Molly-Anne and Susan had a falling out and stopped coming to band meetings, so the fire was snuffed by default.

We were all pretty sad about it, because going to see System Of A Down on Main Street was great fun no matter where you saw them, from the vibe in the room to the parties in the parking lot. I heard that Susan is fronting a Supertramp cover band called The Bloody Well Righteous Brothers, so we might go see them sometime, but nothing can match the joy of watching Kendra "humming a song from 1962."

It meant a lot to System Of A Down on Main Street, and it meant a lot to us. I've never seen Bob Seger perform in person, but I bet that sometimes he gets tired of his songs, forgets why he wrote them. But a cover band, like Rock 'n' Roll itself, never forgets.

Sometimes I wake to the sound of thunder. I wonder if anyone else does?

CHAPTER XI

GOOD MORNING NELLIE OLSEN

Each weekend whilst mowing my lawn
I flash back to the fall of Saigon
And that's not so bad—
Save for all of the plaid
And the fact that "The Waltons" is on.

CHAPTER XII

THE WORLD OF AIDS

WHEN STANDING, PERISCOPE-STYLE, TO VOMIT through the moonroof of a moving prom limousine, Gary Jardiniere advised his teen customers, lest they forfeit the deposit, they should turn around and puke down the back window. It was his experience, as the owner of a 6-vehicle fleet (two of which were Hummers with alternating purple/pink/blue pastel running lights and one a 1979 Lincoln Continental Mark VI that was as sharp and skinny as the coke dealers at John Lennon's funeral), that other vehicles gave his limos a wide berth when approaching from behind, thus no Jardiniere's Livery signs on the back bumper, and that vomit aimed forward or to the side wound up back in the car, ruining Summer.

The type of kids who rented limousines were the type who'd slack off in math if there was no discernible real-world application of it, which is how Gary could keep his prices so high. Same with physics. But even at a cortical, monkey brain level, when all that Aftershock was seeking the cool night air, kids could grasp the arc, the resistance, the force required to heave that vom past the flying V of the tail ornament and maybe, Jardiniere thought, they'd understand in that electrolyte shiver that they'd learned something after all.

Personally, Gary saw no use in limousines. As conveyances for large groups of people they were ridiculous and uncomfortable. Minivans were a superior ride in every way. But such was the cachet of limos to generations of teens intent on gaudiness that he made a killing year after year. A Chinese sound and light system that cost about $450 paid for itself in a weekend. If he threw in a case of hard lemonade he'd make a 300 percent profit on it—kids wanted to appear drunk and they wanted to appear that way in a stretched vehicle.

How quickly wanting to appear drunk reversed itself, Gary thought. From "I'm so wasted" to "I can quit any time." And through the eye of that storm travelled his party limos. From the red-faced football offense and their ovulating dates to the bachelor party (complete with the extra guy to keep the cost down but that no one liked) to the midlife middle manager and a passel of hookers, Gary supplied the wheels for whatever intentions the road was paved with.

For Gary, appearing drunk was not an option, so after each limo was accounted for (occasionally he'd send a couple overnighters to Twisty River or Squanto's Gaming Canopy for the graduates whose parents had given up years ago), he'd drive a leased Kia to his home and tie one on in private: some Johnny Walker Blue or Jameson's Black Label. Bespoke ice cubes in a heavy glass in a darkened room—muted lighting, not like the weaponized strip club array he outfitted his limos with—straight back, five or six in a row, until morning. For maybe 20 years now.

He'd settle into one of two beautiful, throaty leather chairs, the little air pocket between his back and his shirt collapsing unpleasantly in a sweat adhesive, but that feeling would disappear as the petty cares of the day melted away.

"I'm old," he said.

- or some variation. He'd had a wife—Debbie—years ago. Deep down in the last decade. He could no longer recall why they got married or why they divorced. He remembered the particulars of certain dates or certain fights, but never how any of them had felt. At the police auction one Saturday he'd been standing next to a woman for a half hour before he'd put together that she was his ex-wife's maid of honor. He supposed he'd have remembered her sooner if he'd ever bothered to look at the wedding albums. But was there a point in looking? Regardless, he kept them in the garage and pointedly did not throw them out.

One night, just as he was hunkering down to wipe the day away, the doorbell rang. He shifted from Sitting to Standing: Not Without Pain, tapped the small pistol resident in his bathrobe pocket, and approached the front door. Outside stood a stranger.

"Hi," he said to the woman, about 50, wearing a sweater, jeans, and sneakers. Her hair was gray and pulled back. She had glasses with circular National Health frames. Gary's original thought was that she was trouble, that the jeans were a mask and the glasses revealed the real person. He turned out to be right, but he wasn't going to shut the door in a stranger's face, either.

"Hi there!" she said. "So glad you opened up for me. I'm Annmarie Fischer from Trestle Street."

"Gary," said Gary. "What can I do for you, Annmarie?"

"It's Annmarie," she said. "But you're real close!"

Gary was a polite, non-confrontational person by nature. He believed these qualities loaned themselves well to owning a company whose actual usefulness to others he doubted. But he had the urge to just close the door in Ms. Fischer's face at that moment. How many times, as a young salesman, had that same thing been done to him? One of the many nastinesses that he would never do to another human being but that he often saw being perpetrated by others. Oh, like hanging up on a wrong number. The other week Gary got a call on his landline, a man asking for Ray.

"Sorry, there's no Ray here," Gary said, and the caller just hung up on him! Oddly enough, Gary misdialed a number not two days later and, rather than hang up upon the Hello (he was calling the guy from the tire place on his personal line, and a woman answered) -

"Oh, I must have the wrong number," Gary said. "Sorry about that."

"Who are you looking for?" the woman said.

"Armand," Gary said, "but I see that I dialed the wrong - "

"Nope," the woman said, and hung up. It reminded him of the way some drivers would speed up only when they saw you were turn-signaling into their lane.

These things went through his mind, but he didn't slam the door on Annmarie. Instead, he said:

"OK, what can I do for you?"

"May I come in for a moment?" Annmarie said, actively generating air in front of her in her will to move past him. "It's a little breezy and I'd like to talk about something that's happening in the neighborhood."

Well, she was inside, in his chair, smiling at the sparse furnishings, the clearly-unladied furnishings, ratty, unready for guests. He saw in a moment now how embarrassing the surroundings were, when before—when he was alone—they were just perfect.

"Are you a swinging bachelor, Gary?" she asked.

"No, I'm a sedentary one," he said. "I run a limo company."

"Do you occasionally drive the limo?"

"Sometimes I take them in for a wash or a repair," he said, "but mostly I let - "

"There's Syrians all over the neighborhood now," she said. "We've got to close the doors like Hungary did."

"And Texas," Gary added. "But I like their bread."

"And Texas!" Annmarie said. "Are there any particular websites or radio stations you use to get your news?"

"Oh, things pop up on my computer," he said. "The new version of Windows. The news just shows up." He couldn't figure out what her pitch was supposed to be, or when it would assert itself.

"I'm wondering if you've ever heard a radio station called His Word," she said. "It's way down at the left side of the dial. You actually have to turn the knob further than it wants to go and then stick something there to hold it."

"You mean Jesus?"

"No, the radio station," she said. "It's really a wonderful source for news, and recipes, and school closures, sometimes."

"What I meant was, is His Word Jesus's word? Is it like a Bible thing?" Gary said, not wishing he had some device that would make his phone ring and end this interview because he knew she would have just stayed there however long he was on his fake call. Still, there was something about this woman that stirred him a little. He didn't know what it was.

"Oh!" she said. "His Word! I guess it has to be Jesus, right? I just thought that because all the on-air personalities are men that the station was named after them!"

At this point Annmarie unfolded a sleeping mask, put it on, and passed out on his chair. It took so little time before Gary noticed her fingers twitching with REM sleep that he hadn't the presence of mind to tell her to stop. The mask itself moved up and down with the force of her rapid eyeballs.

After a few minutes he sat in the opposite chair, turned on the television, and flipped channels quietly. A few hours later he found a Sharpie, wrote her a quick note on the back of some junk mail, and went to bed. He slept peacefully, deeply. He had not had a drink the night before. Hs head was clear. He felt great.

The next morning he rooted through his closet to find slippers and a robe. Both fit as expected considering he'd not worn such things in more than two decades. He emerged from his bedroom to check on his guest.

But the living room was empty. Annmarie had gone. He looked in the kitchen, expecting to see her there, waiting and smiling, having somehow crafted a breakfast for them out of the odds and ends in his refrigerator. The coffeepot was untouched.

CHAPTER XVII

THE HEART WANTS WHAT IT WANTS II

One autumn I scored me a Groupon
For a trip to the markets of Wuhan
While I wouldn't have missed
My pangolin tryst
My SARS civet's nothing to poop on.

On the kitchen table he recognized the note he'd left her. It had been crossed out by the same Sharpie, and underneath his words were hers:

"Welcome to the world of AIDS!"

He instinctively touched his face, waiting for baby spiders to tumble willy-nilly therefrom. A pre-internet smoking area meme, the "Welcome to the world of AIDS" story was one of a trio of 80's-era cautionary tales about—Gary thought—not using AAA-certified travel agents. A man meets a woman on vacation, they have a lot of sex, she presents him with a little gift box on his departure, telling him to open it on the plane. When he does, he is welcomed to the world of AIDS. Then a woman falls asleep on a foreign beach and a mama spider lays eggs in her face. The woman rubs her cheek with a towel and hundreds of baby tarantulas stream out. Then a guy wakes up in a Sao Paulo tub, short a kidney. Luckily there's a note, in English, instructing him to get to a hospital.

Gary took the morning off from work and got a full STI panel, then had a leisurely breakfast. It was a beautiful day. He decided to walk to work from the diner. It was a hike but he managed. He had a limo take him home.

By force of habit he poured himself a drink, but then saw the note on the kitchen table. He had a feeling that he didn't even have a little AIDS, but the drink didn't seem appealing just then. He poured it back into the bottle, using the note as a funnel. He walked into the living room and saw for the first time the deep indentations his carcass had made in the left-hand chair. He decided to take a walk.

There was something going on with his mood. He couldn't remember the last time he'd felt so light. There was a fluttering in his stomach, a tingling in his face. He felt like he should get a haircut tomorrow.

There was a light spring breeze and the air was warm, wet, and loamy. By chance, way up at the stoplight, he saw one of his Hummer monstrosities cruise past like it was rendezvousing with the mothership. He wondered what it might be like to sell the business, sell the fleet, and travel.

He stopped, fully alive, and stared at the moon. It rose over the distant mountains. He frankly could not believe he didn't know what that range was called.

Brushing the first of what would become hundreds of spiders from his face, he thought, "I'm going to grab a coffee and ask someone."

CHAPTER XIII

WAY OUT YONDER IN THE MEINEKE

"For this muffler a lot I won't pay,"
Cried Edna St. Vincent Millay
"For, 'twixt my clamped thighs
Beaks a pullet surprise
Whose shrieks keep exhaust fumes at bay."

CHAPTER XIV

TICKETS

TICKETS, MY WIFE, was going through some *thing* that I didn't care to have described to me, and I was free as a bird. Through a tacit loophole in an unspoken agreement, I had managed to have delivered unto me, by her, the following items, weekly, and with great bowing and scraping:

1. White Cheddar Cheez-flavored Its, in a bowl, microwaved for about 30 seconds to soften them so that I may break them down with my tongue rather than with my teeth.
2. Softcore teen romps, of the variety featuring older, sadder-but-wiser, date-rapist and slatternly actors playing teens, on DVD with bonus material.
3. Mexican versions of my favorite soft drinks, complete with extra caffeine, worms, peyote, and/or testosterone.
4. All my mail opened for me.
5. A copy of "Lives of the Saints" with the articles taken out.

You might well wonder how my lady suddenly came to her senses to begin treating me with the respect I deserve. Well so did I, but I only thought about it for a second, and then was lucky enough to remember something my brother told me when he got out of rehab: "Streptor," he said, "never think about anything you don't want to get to the bottom of," and by that he meant I should never look a gift horse in the mouth, lest that mouth contain another smaller but infinitely more evil horse.

It started when she got her new job at Anyone for Sauce?, where she made creamy sauces for hotshot businessmen to take home in heated beakers. We'd been fighting a lot recently, the kind of fighting you do when there's nothing left to talk about and you're down to things that annoy you, dinners that are filled with a lot of

Q. What?
A. I didn't say anything.

So she got the job and immediately began to be gone for most of the day, and she would call to say she'd be late, and eventually she just wouldn't call. It allowed me more gripe-free time to play Tekken. She'd come in after I was finished watching whoever do his monologue, and I'd be asleep on the chair. This went on for a few months.

Then, oblivious as I tried to be, I began to notice something. She would dress up for work. Anyone for Sauce?, though it was in the best oxygenated mall down by the synagogues, was still right next to Herbert's Potato World and strictly business casual. Why was she always leaving for work in that bridesmaid's dress?

Then our caller ID box began to be overwhelmed at night. We leave the ringer off so we can screen calls, but I would go to bed with no messages showing and in the morning the thing would be full. No messages, though, so I thought it was some autodialer. But why only at night? Tickets didn't know either. From there it was pretty quick until she missed my nephew's christening due to complaints.

"I'm having complaints," she said.

One of her old friends told me. I heard all the news from them anyway. "Tickets in?" Mellisanie asked over the phone. "Nope," said I. "Oh," she replied, "I guess she's out with Carl, Jr."

I didn't need to be told who Carl, Jr. was. His commercials were on television and his oniony essences were somewhere on my wife's neck. Tickets admitted it pretty quickly, and the funny thing was that everything got better. It was one of those things in a marriage that scientists call a "breakthrough." Was I angry that she was cheating? Hell, no. Was I happy she wasn't eating all the damn Cheez Its? Hell yes.

It's important to put things in perspective, my brother said. Did a satellite fall on your house? No. Did a satellite fall on your house and eat your Cheez Its? Nope. Is your wife cheating on you with the satellite? No. Is your wife cheating on you? Yes. Is she bending over backwards to keep you from suing her or backing over her with a truck?

Yes. Does this remote take double-A batteries? *You know it!*

We've entered a new stage in our relationship. One where the traditional constraints of a healthy marriage needn't be dealt with.

She got Carl, Jr. to commission for me a spoon the size of a welding glove, and then she went out to Costco and got me a pallet of weapons-grade strawberry marshmallow Fluff. I sit in my leathern recliner with my spoonglove on and dig right in. Tickets doesn't hog it away from me because she's been eating healthier lately.

CHAPTER XV

THE HEART WANTS WHAT IT WANTS

No better measure is needed
For a man to feel downright conceited
Than the number of days
His corpse can decay
Before his pets solemnly eat it.

CHAPTER XVI

THE PRINCESS OF COLUMBUS, OHIO

WITH THE LAMENTED PASSING OF Mrs. Millie Klinheuld of Dothan, Alabama, Aramais Sargsyan of Nyack found himself the world's foremost practitioner of "Love Boat" Fan Fiction.

Sargsyan's specialty was the first series, of course. He had never understood the appeal of the late-nineties version with Robert Urich. As the late Mrs. Klinheuld had written at the time in "Exciting And News," Gavin MacLeod's training had been as Murray Slaughter, the affable but no-nonsense newswriter of the "Mary Tyler Moore Show," whereas Urich had played a series of heavies and loners and private detectives. Who would feel comfortable with the haunted Lazarus Man helming the ship?

That was the problem: There were always sage words coming from Mrs. Millie Klinheuld, and Sargsyan had had to put up with years of comparisons. Her "Gopher the Gold" series, in which Fred Grandy and Lauren Tewes take a break from their duties on the Pacific Princess to compete for spots on the U.S. Luge team, cemented her pre-eminence in the field and attracted legions of fans. Sargsyan's own "The New Story of Isaac," in which Ted Lange's father, Abraham (played by Ossie Davis), shows up at a port stop in Puerto Vallarta and attempts to sacrifice Isaac to prove his loyalty to God, was overlooked that year. At the occasional LidoCon when she and Sargsyan would bump into each other, Mrs. Klinheuld always treated him like he was in Steerage. His work had suffered as a result of these snubs. Now, with that Klinheuld monkey off his back, Sargsyan was free to flex his fan fiction muscle.

A year went by and things were going better than expected. Adam Rich and the Dallas Cowboys Cheerleaders had shown up on a special "Fantasy Island"-crossover cruise to save Vicki (Jill Whelan) from the horrors of drinking. He had won, after several years of nominations and inevitable losses to you-know-who, the coveted Brotherhood of the Sea award. His wife had finally agreed to Stubing injections. His new story cycle, featuring the cast shipwrecked on an island in the south Pacific with Jerry Stiller as a wacky tribal chieftain, was receiving critical raves as well as unprecedented popular support.

And that's when his old demon, Depression, began making another run. Sargsyan started feeling like a walk-on character in his own life. He quit his job as a bank teller. He accepted an invitation to speak at the Dallas Lauren Tewes fan club, La Cosa Nostril. For the first time in 19 years, he didn't write his daily episode. Leaving his wife crying at the airport, Sargsyan flew to Dallas in a state of dissolution that would make a poolside bartender blanche.

The convention was eight floors of debauchery. Everyone was dressed as Paul Williams. Paul Williams as Paul Williams. Paul Williams as Cornelius. Paul Williams as Tyrion Lannister. Paul Williams as a tugboat. But always a drunken, half-naked, somehow greased Paul Williams. In whose wild storyline did Paul Williams need to be greased?

When he returned, he was a different man. Rudderless. He sat at his computer, watching his fingers descend upon the keys and then, as if he had nothing to do with it, read words on the screen that meant nothing to him. He had begun an arc involving Dr. Adam Bricker's progressive syphilis and the marooned Doc's inability to quash the advancing spirochetes. He had written himself into a corner.

How many years had he secretly wished for Mrs. Klinheuld's death? Now the laurels were his, and he was screwing up! His wife appeared at the head of the basement stairs. "Come to bed, Armo—I forgive you!" She had never, ever gotten it—who was she to forgive him? This situation required the resolve of a Dick Van Patten, but Aramais Sargsyan would have said "Enough!" at three.

Sargsyan's mind tossed on choppy seas. Fewer and fewer scenarios presented themselves. He was disillusioned: Could it be possible that "Love Boat" fan fiction didn't really matter? He eyed the commemorative ship's compass on the bar, signed by a white-hot Erik Estrada in 1978. Which was the instrument you broke open to drink the mercury and kill yourself?

It didn't matter. He tipped the compass to his mouth.

But at the last minute he thought of his own daughter, Vicki. He needed to be there as she grew. She needed someone to be there when she found out that the Love Boat everyone knew and loved was actually filmed as "The Love Boat II" with a completely different cast from the pilot. She needed to know that Doc—and by extension everyone—could overcome his afflictions.

Sargsyan was inspired. Doc, like himself, had had everything, only to throw it away. Doc's syphilis was a result of his much-ballyhooed sexual prowess. Barbi Benton had guest-starred as a nursing student. Pride had come before Bricker's fall. Now Doc was shambling through tropical underbrush. He blinds himself in a fall. His leg is broken. He reaches the beach in a hurricane, and cries out to God: "Bring me back!"

Evening comes, and morning follows. Sargsyan is pounding away on the keyboard, spinning magic with ClarisWorks 3. Doctor Adam Bricker rouses himself on the sand. He staggers back into the brush. With perseverance and redemptive strength he pulls down a bamboo tree, fashioning sap and bark into two identical spheres, which he smooths with his palms over the next three days. He is lame, pulling himself across the shore with his surgeon's hands, eating only crabs and berries. On the third night he reaches—what do you call it? Satori? Nirvana? Self-actualization?—and prays for forgiveness from his many ex-wives, all the while knowing that they were more at fault than he, but life is too short—and jams the bamboo spheres into his eyes. He is the instrument of his own salvation. He crawls to the beach. Across a shallow inlet he can see them: The Captain, Gopher, Julie, Isaac, Vicki. He calls to them. They come running. So does Don Adams.

Sargsyan clicks File>Save. He shuts down his Centris 610. He goes upstairs where Bridget is waiting with a daiquiri. She never understood, and she never will, but he doesn't care. His mind is on a new romance.

The storm is over, and the Princess glides into peaceful Ensenada.

Moral: The slowed Kopell is saved with wood inventions.

CHAPTER XVIII

THE KIDS GO TO HELL

THE WAY OUT WAS CLEAR. To the left, across the ice, and backwards, sort of, up Satan's frozen upside-down trunk to the foot of Mt. Purgatorio. The gang knew they could do it; Moxie, Mo-Mo, and Batman Murphy had been to Hell and back (well, almost) since they were kids growing up in the hardscrabble streets of Patterson and, in Hamilton's shadow, they vowed that their lives would be exemplary and masterful despite all this crackpot world would throw at them.

"Hey, kid," Moxie said to his girl Mo-Mo, a tough-talking broad with a heart of gold who maybe used a little too much rouge in the bustal area but who otherwise was a standup piece of ass, "be a doll and pull Murph out of that spook's lower left mouth."

The three of them had been everywhere together: Route 66, Middle-earth, the Parisian sewers where Javert sought justice, and nothing could strip the three friends of their plucky American spirit, even as Ring-wraiths dropped barrow-wights on them or Dean and Sal drove over them, time and time again, in their holy goof quest for answers in the Endless American Night or whatever.

Batman Murphy was having a heck of a time up there getting chewed to pieces along with Cassius and the other great traitors. "I shouldn't even be here!" he kept yelling, "I'm only a masturbator!" but Satan just wasn't feeling him. At the top of the triangle in the first mouth, Carl Anderson's Judas Iscariot was writhing away. It occurred to Moxie that depictions of Satan in western literature were hardly ever flattering except, oddly enough, in Black Sabbath's "War Pigs" where the Dark One simply laughs and spreads his wings, like a contented little popinjay.

Here, at the bottom (or top) of the Inferno, Satan, the ultimate Dis, was wedged in ice from his parts down, and topping his shoulders was an unholy trinity of heads with mouths working away at Judas, Brutus, and Cassius. Three sets of eyes wept a bloody froth, despite what one would think would be obvious pride of workmanship. Still, Batman Murphy had managed to get himself caught in a pair of massive plutonian jowls and the crazy kid was looking at an eternity of being chewed up along with that lean and hungry character.

Mo-Mo was doing her best to pull him out but she lacked the leverage. Moxie tried to give her a hand but his palms were all sweaty from their tour through the adulterers' circle. Only Fusaichi Pegasus, the 2000 Kentucky Derby winner, could help them now. Like ZZ Top showing up at just the right time to right small-town wrongs, or the Pony She Named Wildfire coming back out of the blizzard against all odds or, indeed, Brandy finally getting off her own goddamn high horse and marrying one of the many eligible bachelors to whom she served whiskey and wine, the noble 24-year-old pranced gingerly out over one of Satan's three fu-manchus and, gripping Murphy's leg gingerly with perfect teeth, pulled him free of harm.

"Thanks, Fusaichi Pegasus!" cried Murph, handing the well-regarded stud a candy apple, which the latter licked gravely.

But they weren't out yet. All three youngsters climbed onto Fusaichi Pegasus' well-oiled back and shimmied down to Lucifer's hips, each happy that there were so many different ways to refer to the entity they were traveling on. Finally, pressing a secret button he read about in the cheat guide to Quake II, Moxie led his group out of darkness and under the stars.

What was next? Maybe they'd get gig economy jobs selling memes for a buck a terabyte. And after that? Suicide, probably, but who can guess? The three friends and their trusty horse admired the view and one by one lay down to sleep below God's ceiling.

CHAPTER XIX

INVERTING THE CURVE

I fear that I ne'er will climb
From my quarantine habits in time
I do more than Not Dress—
I wholly regress
To a fetid, primordial slime.

CHAPTER XX

ALLEY DOCK

A man with a massive right ball
Had one more two sizes too small
Thus, his signature move
Wore a starboard-side groove
In many a uterine wall.

CHAPTER XXI

WARREN

WE NEVER TOOK HIM SERIOUSLY. Warren was clumsy and perhaps a fool. In eighth grade, completely uncharacteristic of himself, he had crapped his pants in Art class. There were at least two other guys, Francis and Billy, who were known and avoided for just that type of behavior, even to the point that the derision heaped on them had died down to herpetic flareups on special occasions like when the principal, Mr. Joshua, came into the room. Then it would be, "I think Francis needs to go to the bathroom, Mr. Joshua," and "Billy got into the brown fingerpaints again, Mr. Joshua." (One day I was coming back late from band when I saw Mr. Joshua about to go into our room. He was talking with Curley the Janitor and I'm almost sure I heard the principal say, "Why don't you just roll them in sawdust and send them home?").

But when Warren unleashed the dragon in Art, no more was heard about Francis and Billy. In fact, they might have actually stopped crapping their pants after that, having passed the torch as it were. Because Warren was such a damned easy target, it was a welcome relief to drop everyone else's teasing load onto him.

That was how the premature and secretly wonderful Tammy Brogan, who became a woman one morning in gym, got bugged about it for exactly twenty minutes until hapless Warren got himself, one after the other, smacked in the nose with an errant basketball and then accused forevermore of having a period from his face.

I won't not admit to you that Warren and I had an unspoken understanding. At one point I and Spiro were lighting Warren on fire when his mother turned the corner on the way to pick him up. Such was our disrespect that we lit her on fire, too. She screeched and bleated the same way he did, as mother and son did a synchronized roll in some leaves by the water tower, and I wished that his dad had been there too.

Let's get something straight: we were all cruel to Warren. We're all going to Hell. It was only my accidental act of kindness that kept him from turning his pent-up wrath on me.

One day I was playing street hockey with Spiro, Telly, Demo, and Abe Vigoda Jr. Street hockey was a great tension vent after school, and it provided one last chance to nail Warren as he walked down Van Buren Street to meet his mother halfway. We always got there earlier because Warren had to get his eardrops put in by the nurse every day after seventh period. When he would come loping around the corner, trying to remain flush with every branch and hedge in his desire to not be seen, often seeming to flow over them horizontally like rich creamery butter, we would beat him nearly to death with our hockey sticks, slap-shotting street hockey balls into his stomach and high-sticking the brain right out of his head. We should have known that his resilience meant something.

That day I was in a friendly scuffle with Spiro about how his sister, Voula, had fellated the Fire Department. Warren came around the corner and Telly immediately sent a puck right at Warren's face, knocking off his glasses. The glasses flew through the air and, as I was raising my hockey stick to knock Telly's head in for daring to defend his sister's honor, appropriately or not, I happened to connect with Warren's glasses, which I knocked neatly back onto his face. I have never made a shot like that again.

Warren noted this, apparently, and in a sort of falling in love with your kidnapper way he determined I was better than the rest of them. Lucky me. But whereas their deaths came more or less swiftly, I am left to wait out the rest of my life in torment.

That summer Warren began developing muscles. Muscles in strange places. We didn't notice any change in him other than a certain lack of terror as we beat him before school, during lunch, at P.E., and after seventh period. Looking back on it, I should have noticed something was up. There was a glow about Warren, like the glow of knowing the secret of your own redemption. Not only had he discovered a Skill, but alongside that he had also learned to control it.

Warren had developed his sphincter muscles to such a taut intensity that he could rocket-propel his stool through steel walls.

Spiro was the first. At the outset we thought Warren was running away from him. This was odd because Warren had a quality of resignedly lying there and taking it. Spiro began chasing Warren down the street with a hockey stick and Warren ran. It turns out that Warren just wanted to get a good bead on Spiro. It happened so fast I can hardly remember it.

Spiro was getting very angry. Warren's running was winding him. Spiro raised his stick with a vindictive menace; Warren would surely lose some teeth today. Then came the great unveiling.

From the back of Warren's pants came a soft explosion, a <*phoot*!> that sounded innocent enough at that split second but haunts my dreams to this day. Then emerged a corn-studded projectile honed to razor-sharpness that launched itself like an Exocet missile straight for the dumbstruck Greek numbskull. It was over so quickly; Spiro's exit wound was smoking before he hit the ground.

We looked at Warren. He was standing on the mailbox at the corner of Van Buren and Lincoln, staring away from us. I remember thinking, stupid as it may seem now, that he was savoring his victory. But no, that would come later, for he was angling his next shot.

A barrage of ball-bearing-sized mini turds shot through the hole in his Toughskins next. They bounced off the ground about thirty feet away from where Abe Vigoda Jr. and Telly were standing, then cut the boys' heads off with lightning speed. Demo was running now, running faster than I'd ever seen that fat slob run, but with a well-shot cruller Warren severed a tree limb directly over Demo's head and the latter was crushed beneath it.

We were alone, as alone as Warren was every day of his life, but today I shared the shitty silence of his rage. He faced me, and for a split second I thought he was going to shoot fire out of his nipples at me or something, but instead he just adjusted his glasses and walked away.

Turns out Warren did pretty well for himself. He works in the FBI's ballistics lab and has taken that discipline years into the future with his fantastic powers. He was the one, it turns out, who shot down Mir when that satellite was threatening to break its orbit inconveniently over mainland Africa (that one required some PowerBars). He's opened up a set of Holiday Camps, a la Tommy Walker, except Warren's are virtually free of child molestation and pinball. *Virtually*, I say, because they do have that Starship-themed pinball machine, We Tilt This City.

Me, I live with the sadness of the chastened. Children are cruel, and I did cruel, spirit-crushing things. But I was forgiven, and the weight of that sometimes seems crueler (or *cruller*, like what got Demo). Sometimes I dream that I am the President, or a philanthropist, or maybe just the heroic dad to a little family. I am living my life, trying my hardest to do what's right, minding only the business I'm responsible for. I'm the age I am now. Then one day I look up and there's 12-year-old Warren, he's standing in a room, looking out the window. He does not look at me. "I've been waiting for you, Ari," he says, and his buttocks of vengeance pucker briefly and I am smitten with that cleansing fire.

It's not surprising, I think now, how some beings just evolve coping mechanisms that are all about vengeance. That's what the world does to them. But I think it would have been better if Warren had just learned to skate really fast.

CHAPTER XXII

A GOOD HOTEL ON THE ISLAND

Poor Ben Gardner. That sure must've stung.
He should have called "Hey, Aqualung"!
Had he heeded his Tull
There'd be eyes in his skull
Now his corpse is both near and far-flung.

The pictures. It's the first time I remember smiling until my face hurts. In pictures from later years I would frown until my eyes hurt. Some people I know suck in their guts or puff out their chests. That's gotta hurt.

Myrna and I get to school and it's not unlike a place where bombs have been dropped. Screams echo through the varnished wooden halls and there is confusion and crying. And remember that we're all uncomfortably dressed. I see parents nudging their children forward, as if to pay respects at a funeral. The stiff body is the waiting classroom. Myrna is crying, too. I don't know what to do about it. I am grim. I am a grim kid.

Myrna was the first to go. She died in childbirth at 19. Her third child. It was that kind of place. She died a Harvey, not a Babcock-Harvey. Her kids were Kaedyn Stella Harvey, Bryce Cody Harvey, and Hunter Lowell Harvey. The last place we saw "Babcock" was on her grave.

In the classroom are 25 kindergarteners. Lori Dugas is seated next to me. I have never met her before. She is bossy. I quickly learn to raise my hand and wait my turn. I ask Mrs. Walden (it turns out she was never married, but we could not break the habit of calling every woman Mrs.) if Lori might be moved.

"No," Mrs. Walden says. "You and Lori will have to get along."

(Fast-forward to adulthood. Where else but in school and prison must you sit next to someone you don't like, with no option to employ entitlement or other finagling? One can even negotiate a new arrangement on a plane. If I had to give up my childish sense of wonder for the freedom to not sit next to a person who was mean to me, I'd say Fuck Wonder.)

CHAPTER XXIII

THE LONELY VAQUERO

FOR THE BRIEF TIME between the discovery of gold and the arrival of the telegraph, our family was the richest in that village of lean-tos and tearaway shacks. We had a porch, a fence, a domesticated animal. Yes, for about 18 months, Father, Mother, and I were truly content, because things are happiest when one's line of comparison angles downhill.

It was the shaman who told my parents that I would be special, and they didn't know what to do with that information. Manifest Destiny did not trickle down to coddling children. They didn't even know what to do with the shaman. There's this myth that certain cultures have a better way of handling their old leathery people, but we just called him a shaman because Fruit Roll Up with Braids wasn't on our cultural radar.

One day he staggered into our backyard, afflicted with visions. My mother sat him down because he was heading straight for the raised tomato beds. She gave him some coffee and it impressed me even then the way it impresses me now how when you go from nothing to something, the simplest things are just so satisfying. The drunk old fucker bent his face into the cup as if he wanted to absorb the coffee through his eyelids. You can imagine how he felt when my mother stepped out with two heavy pieces of toasted bread with butter and honey on them.

"Heap thanks," he said.

"Whoa. You didn't just say—" my mother said.

"Loretta." my father said. Dad had some moral authority in the town. He was a cooper for a community that was, in a hyphenated word, barrel-happy.

The three of us, plus John, our dog, hunkered around the shaman until it looked like he had come back to himself. I don't know where he got the liquor. Maybe he'd discovered a cache of fermented things out in the wilderness. Anyway, he soon regained some of his clear-eyed crazy that made him the village weirdo, setting aside for a moment the tiresome shambling of the village drunk.

"Your son," he said. "The skinny one with eyelashes like a girl."

"They've only got the one," I said. "I'm right here."

"Your son," he repeated to my parents. "Will be a drug to the Ladies."

"Excuse me?" said my father.

"He will be like ribbons of overlapping beef at a buffet," said the shaman (we didn't have buffets then; I had to look up the word when I got to Cheyenne. I thought there was a Y in it, of course. Everybody did).

"Keep your eye on this one," he said, then fell silent.

The old man eventually left. We would feed him occasionally, but he never elaborated on his prophecy. I'd catch my parents giving me the side-eye sometimes, or looking at me full in the face with a concern I didn't understand.

Shortly afterward, things got bad for us. With the arrival of the telegraph a new cooper blew into town. Back in St. Paul he'd had some success outfitting barrels with a pair of suspenders so that poor people could have something to wear that wasn't rags. It really shone a light on income inequality. But then you'd see people buying those barrel/suspender ensembles and really gussying them up, gluing cheap stones on the outside and lining the interior with velvet. Certain people who were actually fairly well-to-do would play at being poor. My father didn't understand it. He reluctantly cooped a few of the Poor David Suits himself—and each sold within a day—but his heart wasn't in it. People weren't buying barrels to save rainwater anymore. They were instead spending at least three times as much on the latest barrel to be seen in, "begging for alms" to get a laugh from their stupid friends.

Meanwhile the tailor had no orders for new suits, so people who were actually poor would be arrayed in cast-off finery that wealthier people no longer wore. There they were, the unwashed and desperate, looking ill at ease in their silks and high boots, side by side with their cheekboned betters, barreling through town. All we needed were some Visigoths and it would look exactly like Rome in its Decline.

Then there was a stave blight and everything really went to hell.

My mother helped out at the school when my father became so morose that he couldn't function. But then she made the mistake of showing one of the Emory Boys the Cincinnati Method of skinning a rabbit, revealing herself to be an espouser of Comparatively East Coast ideals. She walked right in there, cutting heavy on the flank and skirting the ruff and niblets, like she was kicking up her godless skirts on a steamboat on the Licking. She meant no harm, but that didn't matter. The resulting scandal drove her from the school and made her a community outcast.

My fondest memories of them is how they supported each other in the growing darkness. She was the worse off; neither of them was making money, but at least my father was only unemployed and not also a pariah. They'd hold each other, and sometimes laugh. They'd talk about Ohio like this town had never happened to them.

One night I watched the shaman stumbling up the street toward our place. I held open the rickety gate for him, but he just walked on by. I sat by the raised tomato beds. There was nothing growing. Inside, the house was silent. I called for John, who had taken up watch outside my parents' bedroom. He didn't want to move, but instead stood at attention there. I knocked on their door but there was no answer. John whined.

When I opened the door I was surprised by the relief I felt. Each body twisted slowly, hanging from the main beam. John pawed at my father's feet as if it were a game, but eventually he figured it out. That dog was pretty good with social cues.

I cut them down and laid them on their bed with some difficulty, then called for Deputy Emory. It wasn't lost on either of us that it was his wife who'd made such a fuss about my mother, but neither of us mentioned it. He was respectful. He didn't say anything like, "Well, that's life in the Old West." Besides, my parents weren't the only suicides that month.

He looked around the place. I'd been picking up the slack, so it didn't look too bad. He said, "Are you staying or going? I'll give you ten dollars for the house."

I thought about how far I would have gotten with John on ten dollars. There are those who would have taken the money and shot the dog, booking passage on the next stage out of town. But I was 13 and thought I'd make a go of it. I wasn't going to live with my parents' people—people I'd never met—uninspiring faces staring out of lockets. I imagined I could apprentice myself somewhere, keep my costs low, avoid despair.

"I'm staying," I said.

Deputy Emory handed me a 50-cent piece. I'd spend it plus another dollar on two caskets and a funeral.

I didn't think about it until later, but I lost my parents at just the right age for a post-Civil War/Western Expansion kid. Life expectancies were low so there wasn't that boomerang return of parental reconciliation where you'd walk among the trees with your dad or where you and your mom would grasp oversized, steaming cups of tea in two hands as the rain misted the windows and you ovulated. Successful or no, there was a good chance my parents would have dropped dead of natural causes in a few years if they hadn't eased themselves out.

I was taken into the service of Mr. Lazarus, the banker, and we quickly discovered that I was facile with numbers and recordkeeping. He taught me how to fire a gun and I was surprised to learn that I enjoyed brandishing it to thwart would-be robbers. Our little bank grew. I even installed one of my father's old barrels out front and turned it into a flower pot. The barrels-as-clothing craze had died down and I found myself earning extra money by making planters in my father's coopery. I wondered what he would think of my work.

I don't even recall him calling it a coopery.

John was about 12 when he died. He'd been sleeping beneath my feet at the bank. From my stool, my feet dangled above his head. When it happened, he gave one final, friendly swat at the toe of my shoe. I asked Mr. Lazarus for a half hour so I could go bury my dog.

And that's when it happened. I was walking down the center of the rutted, muddy track toward Romulus Hill. It's where the cemetery would be for the next 25 years, and suddenly the Widow Becky was staring at me frankly.

"John's dead," she breathed.

"I'm taking him up Romulus Hill," I said, holding 70 pounds of stiff dead dog in my arms. "I'm burying him next to my parents."

"He sure was a good dog," said the Widow Becky, looking me straight in the eye. "Vigorous."

I didn't know what was happening or why the Widow Becky was talking to me this way. I looked at the ground and saw that she was making little quarter-circles in the dirt with her heels. I felt flushed, possessed by something. And yet I was also aware that this was a feeling I could master, the way I had percentages, compound interest, and drawing multiple thick, efficient parallel rules across ledger pages.

It seemed as if John took a posthumous breath, egging me on. I regarded the Widow Becky, recalling how all the right parts were pressed against the cylinder of her black funeral barrel just weeks before.

"This'll be the third grave I've dug," I said. "It's sweaty work. And I might cry."

"My root cellar is dank and inviting," the Widow Becky said. "I keep a cool milk goat down there when the days are sultry."

"I bet you do," I said. It was as if restless sand worms were coiling and uncoiling under the cheap fabric of her dress. The Widow Becky was at a standing writhe.

"Do you need help committing your loyal dog's body to the earth?" she asked.

"I would like that," I said. "I don't know a grave from a hole in the ground."

"I thought you said you dug your parents' graves," the Widow Becky said, archly.

"I was a child then, but now I'm a man," I said, taking her wrist and squeezing it, imparting meaning in a way I didn't know existed. "So I forgot."

"Everyone knows how to dig a grave," she said. "You just—"

—but our steamy tete-a-tete was interrupted by a lithe, erotic jerky stick of a woman who'd departed the Post Office, crossed the road, and heaved a bundle of burlap into the Widow Becky's face, then leapt upon the stunned woman and pinned her in the muck, pummeling her nearly unconscious.

"You're talking too familiar!" the second woman said, grabbing fistfuls of the Widow Becky's hair.

The Widow, meanwhile, scooted backward enough to land a kick in the thin woman's throat. An instant later, both were supine in the filth, breathing heavily.

A crowd had gathered. The menfolk—this is what we call a group of men that is not fighting— regarded me thoughtfully. A few of the women stood in their sweaty, straining frocks, violently grooming their wiggling children.

To the Widow Becky and her sinewy assailant I found myself saying for the first time something I'd have occasion to repeat often:

"Ladies, *Ladies*—please don't fight."

I climbed the hill to bury John. The warm earth was yielding in the early summer. I eased him down into the hole and rhythmically loamed on top of him, heavy and warm and wet. I turned to find the ladies of the village behind me, each grasping a casserole dish, or a cobbler, or a pitcher of cream, or some blackberries, or—and it took me a while to understand this—a full complement of horse tack including the two types of martingales: driving and riding. The women had come to a truce.

During the next month the air was charged with ozone and essences. On Mr. Lazarus's advice I sent away to Belgium for a manual. By the time I got past the italicized Roman Numeral pages and into the book's meat, commerce had ceased in the town. Mr. Lazarus took me aside.

"You've been nothing but an outstanding employee," he said, "but the arrival of your Gift has been like an algae bloom in our inland waterways. Men like you can't live among upright people. You drive them bats. Sooner or later one of these men is going to forget your daddy and your good work and take a shovel to you."

I knew he was right. I looked at the town center. The women kept their distance but within a hundred feet there were at least a dozen of them winding around hitching posts, porch supports, and the discarded leg of a Colossus the town lyceum had hoped to erect before it ran out of funds.

That night I left my home. I had some savings plus a few dollars from Mr. Lazarus and several of my parents' friends. I saddled up an old paint and crested Remus Hill, looking back at the house my parents built, the bank, the myriad places where I and the women of the village, old and young, had arrived at an understanding. I noticed the shaman weaving his way up his own hill on the opposite end of the valley, and wondered what had tipped him off.

CHAPTER XXIV

INHERITANCE

I don't know which parent to thank
For my powerful Musteline stank
Which leaks from my sacs
When faced with grim facts
(e.g. when I go to the bank).

CHAPTER XXV

NOW THEY'RE ALL DEAD.

WHAT'S THE FIRST THING you remember? I was old enough to remember, and retain the memory, by then. A cool morning, summer definitely over, but very bright. Why? Because I am up early. The sun is in the east, and so am I. The first morning of kindergarten, 50 years ago today.

It is even earlier than usual, because we have to take pictures. Those pictures survive, each one of them poorly composed, blurry, with squinty subjects, half-smiling or over-smiling. There were maybe 12 exposures in the film cartridge back then, right? So every shot had to mean something, and none of them ever did.

Each item of apparel on my thin frame is new. Not just for that year, but for my life. Why would I have needed a cardigan sweater before? Every piece of clothing chafes, and I can smell the chemicals that made my pants.

I'm standing with Myrna Babcock. It's her first day of school, too. 50 years pass and names like that just get erased. No self-respecting person would even be named Babcock these days. It's not the same, but go to Germany and see how many Hitlers are left. Those names just die out.

Lori passed away three years ago when she was hit with her husband's boat while waterskiing in New Hampshire. Mrs. Walden died alone in 1991. My mother sent me the obituary. Some moms really throw themselves into clipping obituaries and mailing them.

At recess is Johnny Logiudice. Dead at 26. Danny Savard. Dead at 28. Then a lot of people who died just last year: The Voulas Spirodakis and Jeannakis, Billy Lambert, Scotty Murphy, three Heathers and four Stephanies, Tracy Klippin, Brian Everett (the most celebrated death: he was taking pictures of one of the mills being torn down and *was crushed by the chimney*), Jennifer McMartin, the mayor's daughter and my first kiss (she stayed thin and athletic all her life and moved to Santa Barbara; we almost met when I was out there for a conference, both of us between marriages in our 30's, but it never worked out), dead of an aneurysm, Molly Sheehy, Ari Kaplan, Beverly Parreira, Georgie Panagiatakos. All of them between 42 and 44 when they exited through the cloakroom.

Finally there are the twins, Robby and Roddy Lebow, sons of the cantor. They killed each other. It is officially a death by misadventure, but they were 35 and childless, lived with each other after Robby's divorce, stayed in town in Roddy's house. They eventually moved into the one room that wasn't piled with newspapers. Then one day, someone lit a match. They were found side by side, the one or two documents that would mean anything in a fireproof box under Robby's bed.

Robby and Roddy notwithstanding, we didn't light the world on fire, did we? One of the Stephanies was a city councilor in Minnesota, but that's how high our ladder extended. It's true that it's way too early, statistically, for this many of us to be dead, but no one is amending an actuarial textbook because of us, commissioning a study, or even asking me to tell my story on a podcast (and there are so many podcasts).

When I go, I'll be the last to remember Myrna Babcock's face on that first day of kindergarten. We both turn into the cloakroom and are briefly alone. It is a dark, thin wooden room with heavy iron coat hooks. The way she lifts her arms to place her lunchbox on a shelf gives me an idea of what she'll look like when she's older. That is new to me. Her future self looks a lot like her mother, but so much more beautiful. She is crying.

"It'll be O.K., Myrna," I say.

She seizes my hand and holds it, for a moment, before I pull it away.

CHAPTER XXVI

ANCIENT CHINESE SECRET

Division of laundry made strides
'Ere Brutus and his regicides
In bleached togas slew
Stains with Et Clorox II
(Which is where we get "Whites of their Ides.")

CHAPTER XXVII

STRIKE VECTOR MATRIX

WE WAITED FOR THE appointed hour, and then we struck. A thin, tight line of mercenaries moving swiftly under the eaves of the riverside forest and its railroad trellises. I was the leader, and there was Rhondat, a brassy waitress with kind eyes, Duke, a jaded private detective who still had friends on the force, Nero, a kindly (and spiritual!) old black man who could burn things with his mind, Sled, a doomed loner, and Bonky, our sidekick with Downs Syndrome and a smile. We made good time as we headed downstream, silvery figures in the moonlight, toward our destination.

We had been called out of a life of legitimacy for one final score (except for Nero, who was just about to retire and was getting too old for this). I was summoned to the undersea lair of Mr. Porthole, deformed billionaire genius, and was told to assemble the old gang for the last time. Our mission: This time it was personal. Mr. Porthole's virginal but stacked daughter, Dusty, had been kidnapped by evildoers whose nationality changed every week. Dusty meant everything to Mr. Porthole, whose wife, the brilliant scientist Brandy Grey, had died tragically of a disease so rare it ceased to exist after it killed her. Her death came mere hours after the delivery of her only child, Dusty.

"You've got to help me, Ray," Mr. Porthole said as he turned his chair to face me and took off his glasses, all the while straightening some papers on his desk. I was a loose cannon pilot ace, the only man ever to be in Delta Force, the Navy Seals, the French Foreign Legion, and Van Halen at the same time. My three Congressional Medals of Honor bumped shinily against my massive chest, more robust than a woman's. I could see my old friend was in despair, his broad, still-muscular shoulders shaking with rage and desperation, his hideous body heaving in the wheelchair, the silver at his temples.

In the next room Miss Acheson, a handsome woman, pined for him and did his filing.

I stood while my old friend recited my accomplishments.

"Ray Blood. Eagle Scout, Navy Cross, postgrad at Stanford, Rhodes Scholar, Judo Champion, Astronaut, Pike's Place Fishmonger. Elektra Recording Artist. I need you, Ray."

"I'd forgotten about 'One by Mouth (The Night),'" I said.

"That was a triumphant Teen Choice Awards," Porthole said. "You won it all."

Still, I had to be honest with him, because I always shot from the hip: "John, my marriage was on the rocks before I quit this job; I wasn't seeing my daughter grow up—I was too busy chasing around the world for you, fighting crimes my way and dispensing justice, Ray Blood-style, which, as you know, is Puget Justice."

Mr. Porthole said, "I know all this, Ray, but Dusty is all I have left."

Put that way, I realized that my marriage and family were less important than my friendship and whatever unspecified relationship he had with his daughter. I got the gang together in a series of montage-sequence adventures: Rhondat from her secure but unfulfilling life as a secretary, Duke from his secure but unfulfilling life fishing in Nevada with his decades-younger wayward wife, Nero from his secure but unfulfilling life in the circus shoveling up after the elephants, Sled from his secure but unfulfilling life as an Instagram influencer, and Bonky from his secure and retarded life scaring women as they walked over Japanese garden footbridges. As each teammate walked away from stability, he or she made sure to throw something on the ground—an apron, a cap, a fishing rod, his own stool—saying "I quit!"

Only I knew how to inspire them.

Mr. Porthole gave us blueprints of the facility where Dusty was being held for ransom or worse, and a detailed map of the area. The crew met at midnight, all looking a little out of shape, but after some calisthenics, Sled's being revealed as a traitor, and his last-minute deathbed renunciation of his treacherous intent, they all looked fit and trim, except Bonky, who nonetheless kept his leg warmers on for the rest of the mission, which made us all laugh.

As I left our houseboat on the bayou, my wife had said, "The kid and I might not be here when you get back." I replied with a not-casual mention of who this job was for, and that Mr. Porthole worked for America, so I was not only proud but downright obliged to subcontract for him. This fact made her reconsider, and she wagged one long leg at me from the silky recesses of her kimono. Now she said, "When you come back, I'll be naked and our daughter will have been sent somewhere." I kissed her hard.

Strike Vector Matrix raced toward the heavily-guarded, quasi-military installation. Rhondat gave us all some no-nonsense advice for the lovelorn, Duke got himself a sock in the jaw from some bruiser whose dame Duke had made a play for, Nero brought down the flames of righteousness, and Bonky touched us all with the tale of his love for a lonely, bespectacled secretary he saw walking by his group home every day.

It's not important how we saved Dusty. It is only necessary to know that the leader of the terrorist mob was killed last, right after he revealed that Dusty's kidnapping was a result of his own jealousy of Dusty's father for the unrequited love of Dusty's mother. I killed him in a way that allowed for his final screams to trail off as he fell down a chasm or something. I forget. I got a scar on my face that will remind me of all this, but luckily my wife was waiting at the shipyard for me, wearing a broad-rimmed sunhat and toting a fellating.

As we parted, Mr. Porthole embraced me warmly but masculinely and said, "Is there any way you might come back to work for us, Ray? You know you're the best."

"Maybe," I replied, walking arm in arm with my wife to an idling Mustang, "but we're going to take a long-overdue honeymoon." Everybody laughed for some reason and, validating something old Nero had said earlier, their faces froze that way.

CHAPTER XXVIII

MARY OLIVER & H.P. LOVECRAFT NEVER HAD A 2ND DATE

The poetess bade me but lay
My jortsed man-frame down in the hay
But later I'd birth
A Thing Not of This Earth
(A Grasshopper used me That Day.)

CHAPTER XXIX

THE MASQUE OF THE RED DEATH II

BECKY, LIKE KETCHUP IN A MIRROR, was beside herself with anticipation. This would be the best party ever. Everyone from the society she longed to be part of would be there, and they would all be looking at her. This was the culmination of months of work, and nothing could go wrong.

Oh, the wonderful plans! A life-size depiction of the wreck of the Edmund Fitzgerald would be created entirely in cats, right down to the sea foam Manxes on dirty Lake Superior. At "Does anyone know where the love of God goes?", the USC marching band would play "Tusk" for 24 hours straight. A barbershop quartet would entertain for the first hour, be castrated, and then perform nuts-free for the serving of dinner. And the dinner! There would be 33 courses, a la the gala dinners of the Sultan of Larribird back in the oughts, and served by rollerskating robots with filthy minds, bearing trays of sliced goose, rock candy, jelly rolls, Pomeranian bitch ova, kosher salt from the Sea of Tranquility, clam donuts, vampire oranges, greased cherubim with a full arm up the ass, Tab, Veal McNuggets, the blood of the firstborn, yam scampi, tater pubescents (for the flavor), braised little donkey, chaff-infused wheat, Cap'n Crunch with ex'ra Cap'n, Froot flavored Loops, zucchini neckties, creamed Andes Mints, shepherd's pie with real sheep, manta rays, nebulous crabs, blush wine, elfin *lembas*, chocolate-covered swarms of bees, ham sandwiches, whole vitamin D milk, adam's apples from the criminally insane, Sweet Tarts, non-diet Spree, cream of broccoli soup with a noggin in it, peach cobbler, and a hard-boiled egg. The tables were laid out, it seemed, for miles.

But Becky fretted; where was her suitor, the dashing Count Nibs? He had been on a fox hunt earlier and had scared the fox so badly that the creature had wet its bed, but surely her betrothed would be done by now? She stood at the bay window, her hooped skirt backing up traffic all the way up Spit Brook and left on Daniel Webster, and watched the rolling fields that laid themselves at the foot of Cutlery, the mansion that had been in her family for hundreds of years. He would come.

She had never known of a guest list that was so complete. Not a single regret or cancellation! Every one of her 400 invitations had been accepted within days. That made it so much easier—but wasn't it a rule of thumb that at least 15 percent would not arrive? Becky bet that tonight, that skank-ass rule of thumb would get slammed in the door of her Lexus. She knew that, within hours, the halls of Cutlery would be ringing with the gay voices of all 400 of her invited guests, and all would return to their homes with that wonderful combination of satisfaction and envy that was the hallmark of good parties.

The butlers and maids hurried this way and that, hoisting the butter statue of her and the Count 150 feet above the grand hall, lubing the luge for later, and stapling peacocks under certain seats as prizes. When the Bimblemann-Smythes appeared with their entourage, Becky knew that somehow her Franco had encountered trouble but seated her first guests with great aplomb and not a hint of the worry that was beginning to gnaw at her.

Soon arrived the Trent-Warblies, the sugar-substitute barons, the Mr. Jack Solonoids of Clampett, the empress dowager Bootsie, Chlamydia Venus-Lather the eminent lady chiropodist, and the headless elk boy. They were joined by Cardinal Fizzy Flimptitoots of Chicago and his delightful wife Carl, a family of dogs from the neighborhood, and a suspect group from the seminary called Men2Boys. The remaining guests glided in, looking uniformly grand, but never did Becky betray her fear that something horrible had happened to the good Count. Still, no one mentioned him. Did they know?

At 1 a.m. the less-hardy guests had begun to depart, stopping to kiss their lovely hostess or press her hand warmly, feeling an age-old desire to be on the edge of seventeen as well as to thank her physically, somehow, in addition to verbally, for the wonderful time Becky had made possible for them. At 4 a.m. the last of the guests had staggered out. Her photo would be in all tomorrow's papers up and down the east coast, smiling cryptically at readers in their bathrobes and shirtsleeves who could never know such complete and utter fabulousness. And yet Becky was morose.

It was at 6 in the morning, when she had just decided to at least phone the police, that the Count arrived. He rode his Nine-Hand Tennessee Fluffy up to her door, allowing the horse to knock with its brass-tipped tongue. Becky, butter having fallen on her tresses like a bread commercial, threw open the door.

"Sorry I'm late," he said, "I decided to get a job vacuuming the carpets up at the country club. It might be fun for the summer."

"You were vacuuming all last night?" Becky asked, incredulous.

"No," he replied, "I was making out with your old gym teacher. She's got thighs that could crack a fire hydrant."

Becky collapsed into the structure of her skirt. A *job*?

CHAPTER XXX

THE LONELY DAUPHIN

His mom, wishing he'd been Chinese
Bound his feet like a half sleeve of peas
Hobbling in socks the
Munchausen's by Proxy
Child was consumed with unease.

CHAPTER XXXI

ELEGANT SPACE GENTLEMAN

I DON'T KNOW MUCH about theology, but I know what I like. I'd been having this waking fantasy while doing the dishes or strolling through the produce aisle: What if Jesus were real? What if He was as groovy as He looked? What if He were some kind of astronaut?

It made sense that, if He ever existed in Zero A.D. Jerusalem, He'd be runty and brownish by our standards, a Dachshund compared to the Golden Retriever you see in The Watchtower. I'd been brought up with the American Jesus, a Barry Gibb-looking Dude with blow-dried hair and a heartlight. This was a Jesus Who, when asked "How Deep Is Your Love?" would answer: "*Balls Deep.*" Truly the Greatest Salesman in the World with the motto *Always Bee Gee Closing.*

I never understood the devout for this reason. If Jesus existed, He'd have looked like their gardener. But Chamber of Commerce Jesus—that shot of Him opening His shirt to reveal a radiant, bleeding heart? Exquisite. It was like a celestial Teen Beat layout. You think their gardener would have gotten past the first button? Of course not. People should come to terms with the fact that the resurrection and Western Civilization itself would not have happened had Jesus actually looked like Barry Gibb.

"Stayin' Alive" was not a work of irony.

What was a conundrum was that modern technology had made it possible for *anyone* to look like the Children's Bible Jesus. All a fellow needed was the leisure time to blow out his hair and pay attention to his teeth. But if he, all Christed up, then strolled into some Bible study he'd be arrested for vagrancy, clean robes or no. This Lady-Friendly Sensitive Stud created by greeting card companies and the YMCA was a Walking (on water) Contradiction. If Jesus comes back, He'll be deported to Burning Man.

That's why I never sought out a personal connection with the Lord. Too many mysterious ways.

I once brought a boyfriend home for Thanksgiving. I'd met him at school. His parents lived in New Mexico and no one could afford the plane fare, so there he was on the porch of our place in Connecticut.

"Just be Yourself," I said, already imagining the ways I'd regret it.

There was no way he was getting out of there unscathed. He was wearing some Baja pullover he'd got at the Student Union for 10 bucks, his hair was long and beatific, he'd grown this stupid freshman beard because he could, and he looked so serene that sometimes even I wanted to punch him in the face. I made sure we were both visible under the porch light lest my father never open the door at all.

"This is Alan," I said to my unblinking parents.

"Thanks so much for inviting me," Alan said, extending his hands, palms up, as if he expected to ascend then and there.

"Oh, it was Karen who invited you," said my father, half way already to the downstairs bathroom from which we'd be sure to hear The Works.

My mother made small talk. She may have been putting on a show for my younger brother, who hadn't moved from the couch and his Xbox game to greet us. Alan told her his major was Religious Studies.

"What more do you need to know that you haven't already learned in church?" she asked helpfully. She bustled about the kitchen. She could make doing nothing look exhausting.

Alan should have answered that the Bible was so fascinating and rich that he wanted to study it with the best minds in the country (which would have been true). Instead he said that everyone from the Jews to the Muslims to devotees of some West African corn god had something to tell us about the human condition. Mom placed a hand on the counter to steady herself. From the bathroom, Dad let out something sonorous and submarine.

"I'm going to tell Karen's father that you study Science," my mother told Alan. Since Alan was in a shameful degree program, concealing it from my father would be their little secret. "That will be better."

Alan got along with my brother and even made my father laugh. My mother was taken with him in spite of knowing the embarrassing truth. As I led him to the guest room, he tried to kiss me. I wouldn't let him.

"Not here," I said.

But I could hear him in the next room as I got into bed. We'd done so well with my parents. It would be such a waste if we blew it on something so scandalous. I tiptoed to his room anyway.

"Do you have everything you need?" I asked.

"No," he said.

"What is it that - ?" Oh. I got it.

"How polite should I be," he asked, "at any given time?"

"Just until Sunday," I said.

"I see the next three days stretching out forever," he said.

I stood in the doorway as he turned over, dismissing me.

"Good night, Alan," I said, loud enough so my parents would know I was saying good night. He said nothing. I walked back to my room, treading heavily on the runner in the middle of the floor. They'd hear me walking. I paused at my door, reached into my room, turned the light off, and closed the door from outside. I tiptoed along the wall where the floor wasn't squeaky and was back in Alan's room in less than 30 seconds.

"Stop pretending," he said.

"I'm here now," I said.

He turned to face me in the darkness. I saw the moisture of his eyes.

"Karen," he whispered.

"Shut up. Shut up, Alan." I got under the covers of the ridiculous twin bed.

"No, Karen," he said, pushing me away gently. "I've got the stigmata."

There were some other girls in the dorm who'd dated Alan, and yes, we talked. My roommate, Liesl, had explained it like it was a period, except, you know, five separate places.

"He gets moody," she'd said. "He retreats."

I admit that I'd been curious. I wanted to see it. In ninth grade there was a boy with Klinefelter's Syndrome but that wasn't much of a payoff. But this.

"He got one during Pledge Week when no one could get any sleep," Liesl had said. "It's stress-related."

I couldn't help myself. I threw off the covers. Alan hid for a moment, then relaxed and opened up. He was crying softly. He lay there as I inspected his hands, feet, and side. The wounds were clean and free-flowing, and smelled like vanilla. Luckily it wasn't Projectile Stigmata, otherwise there'd be more to sneak down to the laundry tomorrow than just the sheets. But it was still fascinating. Eventually he calmed down, pale blue light shining from each hole.

"This happens sometimes," he murmured. I knew. Quindreth, who lived at the other end of the hall from me, had gotten drunk with Alan one night and they sort of fell into bed together. He was respectful, she said, but it took some effort. They were both pretty wrecked anyway. She got up to go to the bathroom around 5 a.m. and saw that he'd stigmataed on her cervical pillow and stuffed animals. She woke him up and told him he was Gross.

Now that I saw it happening, the excitement had dimmed. Sure I hadn't seen anything like that before in real life, but now that I had, it seemed more like a liability to any future relationship with Alan. The certainty of that stood in relief to the way I'd felt before. I just turned off, despite feeling a twinge of accomplishment that I'd made someone stigmata himself in my childhood bed.

I guess he knew I'd made my decision—people like that tend to know—and things got colder. But what could we do? He put his face in the pillow as I tiptoed back out.

He made some noise about heading back to school on the bus, but in the end it was just easier to have him stay. We took a walk and watched a couple of movies, but he mostly ended up on the couch with my brother playing videogames. My father seemed satisfied that we weren't together.

"Not working out with you and the Messiah?" he asked me.

The following Sunday we returned to school, barely speaking. The moment hadn't brought us together, maybe because I hadn't gone on a journey of my own. I hadn't revealed anything; Alan hadn't witnessed any spectacle he hadn't generated himself.

I didn't talk to him again until just before Spring Break. We'd managed to not be in the same room for three months. I bumped into him coming out of the library. We hugged and he asked me how I was doing. I was OK, I said, I was seeing someone—one of the teaching assistants! I told Alan like it was confession—and we were going to Myrtle Beach for the break. Alan was going to build houses in Appalachia.

"Ooh, a carpenter," I said. "You and your nails."

He didn't come back. I found out on Facebook that he'd ditched Religious Studies and transferred to MIT, of all places, where he eventually earned his doctorate in Planetary Science. In 2023 he'd been selected for the crew of the first manned Orion mission. Liesl had scored an invite to his going away party, negotiating clearance to travel to a facility at Edwards Air Force Base. She was married, he'd been celibate since freshman year in college (Liesl was his first and last), but they'd remained friends.

She'd asked him if he ever came down with stigmata again.

"Everybody's got something," Alan had said thickly. "They almost replaced Lieutenant Commander Scoggins because she has gout."

We watched the launch on CNN, the sleek bird twisting like a corkscrew. It pierced the clouds and was gone, and that was farewell for Alan. It was like the Irish Wake, where sending the boys off to America or Australia meant saying goodbye forever—a living death. We permanently part ways with hundreds of people a month, I imagine, but it's rare we can say with any certainty that we will never see someone again. That's what makes it special.

"I wonder if he was ever happy," Liesl said.

30 years later they fished a battered Bucky Ball out of the Indian Ocean, just as planned. The sphere was scored like the pots at a soup kitchen, but the contents were in perfect condition. The crew of the Orion had jettisoned the boxcar-sized Ball and used Mars' orbit to slingshot it back. On a spring day in 2054 I was invited to the Jet Propulsion Laboratory for a lunch. I recognized some of the crewmembers' relatives, as well as Liesl's son, Tony. It turns out there were some personal effects in the Ball that pertained to each of us. A 2-star General presented me with a medium-sized box with Alan's freshman picture on

the cover. Inside was the Baja pullover and a pillowcase with his blood on it. I recognized his face in the blood.

"This is so gross," said Tony, who'd received a similar pillowcase blood profile in honor of his late mother. "Did he just go up there with a bunch of bags of laundry?"

The lunch was very tasty and I went home with the box as well as a few high-quality flight jackets for my grandsons. I didn't know where to put the pillowcase, but the reporter from the paper who came out to interview me suggested I donate it to our old school, and that's what I did.

I'm not certain it was me who'd inspired Alan to slip the surly bonds of earth so I could touch the pillowcase. I still remember the feeling of having dodged a bullet that night in my old room. But now I wonder if I'd been made to play some role in Alan's journey to Space and The Infinite. In darker times I feel less like myself, a woman with degrees and a career and grandchildren, and more like some faceless character the hero is supposed to meet in a fable.

It's uncomfortable, I guess, but if things were easy we'd all just stop getting up in the morning.

CHAPTER XXXII

A GOOD HOTEL ON SOLARIS

Whatever you do, please don't take
The boat on the sentient lake
Once it gets in your head
You'll wet more than the bed
So just give Housekeeping a break.

CHAPTER XXXIII

THE DROUGHT AND THE SINK

RAY WOKE FACE DOWN, IN the park, his mouth full of municipal verdure; rampant, incidental greenth, on a warm spring morning, unhurried by police or pissing dogs, non-hassled. He got up, creakless, clearheaded, appearing to any casual observer like someone just pausing from a jog. He thought, I don't look like the Creative Commons-sanctioned portrait of someone who passes out in the park. He walked across the street to get a hot dog and some coffee.

*****

20 years later he was on another side of the country, coasting up the driveway and hearing the rubber on the cement, the rubber yearning to become one with the cement in this, the fifth year of a drought. To the right, the lush, turved verge of the building some flippers just bought. To the left, the lack-of-grass surrounding his own place. Ground-level basement windows askew, inviting skunks in to die and decompose, wires from decades of former tenants' cable companies snaking up to a roof only visited by generations of cable guys. Squalorville. It must look like the lunar surface up there, Ray thought, after the Apollo missions' mom had simply refused to clean up their shit anymore.

Into the garage drove Ray, and he walked out into a wall of heat. A quick cross to the back door and into the not-necessarily-cool (but dark) tail end of the house. There he paused and heard, from the heart of the home he shared with Audrey, water running.

It ran unhindered, in a tight free fall, straight into the drain. It was a torrent, he would see later, that fell between dishes but not on them. Audrey stood at the sink rehearsing an argument she would have with someone—perhaps Ray—later. When he discovered her in these soliloquies he would call her Lady MacNugget, but not out loud. She was saying:

"And I take care of the kid. And you're not here. And I make lunch. And there's only so much patience that I have. I start the day with a full bucket of patience. Then the bucket is empty. It's empty! It's empty. So of course I put her in front of the TV! Because I can't play pretend games with her all day. I can't! I can't. And I can't be cheating on you simply by sharing emotional intimacy with other people. You're tomcatting around with your hands full of Tawny's tits."

Oh boy, Ray thought. I guess this one's for me.

Because last week he heard:

"And you have to have fresh-cut flowers every day? And you complain about there not being enough money? But you have to have fresh-cut flowers. You have to have them! You have to have them. No wonder he wants nothing to do with you. You should really find a 12-step program that will help you with this. You can find a lot of peace in the Rooms."

(That was for her best friend.)

Or:

"Secret smoker. Secret alcoholic. Sure! You did that. What kind of wife were you? He had to sneak away to do those things because you were always sniffing around and couldn't let him be. Couldn't let him be! Couldn't let him be."

(Her mother.)

Ray paused in the hallway. He thought that listening to her practice an argument was like reading her diary, going through her emails. He usually told her when she'd start talking to herself. Sometimes he'd hear her in the bathroom or she'd do it on long car rides. Her mind just settled into grievance position. He thought of the firemen on the old locomotives, shoveling coal into the furnace, except she was shoveling her friends under a bus. And other metaphors.

When he commented on it, she'd tell him there wasn't a woman she knew who didn't work things out that way.

"Do you think Hillary Clinton does it?" he asked, reconsidering his vote.

"Of course she does."

He knew the rhythms he fell into when he washed the dishes. He'd start reciting "Rappers' Delight" or "Baby Got Back" or "Ya Got Trouble." He was just pissed she wasn't actually washing any dishes during these speeches, with California's future going straight down the drain. Didn't she know there was a drought on?

He backed up, deciding to go out and come in again.

Back in the driveway he felt the sun on his bare scalp, cooking it, cooking the mucus of a spring cold. Ugh. He remembered a place filled with effortless green, where having a cold made sense. It was easy to be phlegmatic in a place where your cold made sense.

He thought about Tawny's tits. She'd just got new ones and was putting them in everyone's hands. Ray's weren't special. Whoever the photographer was, she had easily 50 pictures of men and women holding Tawny's New Boobs. Ray would have done the same thing if he'd gotten a new Sno-Cone machine. Was he supposed to have pushed Tawny's tits away? Or—what if?—maybe never put himself in a place where Tawny's tits would be anywhere near him? Like Tennessee?

He walked back into the house. "Honey! I'm home," he said. From the kitchen he could hear the faucet being turned off.

Did they all become Audrey eventually? No. Now and then there was a Jean, or a Nikol, or—let's face it—a Tawny. Could Ray be Ray without an Audrey?

This Audrey finished Ray's sentences but 90 percent of the time got the endings wrong. This Audrey pretty much resented everyone she knew and spent her free time rehearsing zingers that may or may not get delivered. This Audrey, Ray was very sure, was going to be a *terrorist* during menopause.

And another thing. Ray had once loved this Audrey, so there was that, too.

*****

A year later, Ray looked at his misspelled name on the coffee cup, and began to harbor doubts about the barista's grasp of How Things Are. What nailed it was when she said, "You two are such a cute couple!"

Ray glanced at Audrey, who was playing solitaire on her phone a few yards away, and said, "I am very lucky, thank you." He dropped a tip into the plastic thing and returned to his soon-to-be ex wife and said, "That's funny—the barista just called - "

" - out sick, yeah," Audrey said, not looking up. "That's what happens when you don't pay a living wage."

They were in for a day of meetings with lawyers and accountants, finalizing the dissolution of a marriage that, oh my god, never should have happened.

He hadn't had coffee for a while. That first cup after abstaining always made him feel great. It put him in mind of that morning, about 20 years ago, when he'd woken up in Central Park after basically passing out in the grass after a party. It had not been the smartest thing to do, but he awoke refreshed and unmolested, cash in his pocket. He'd walked jauntily across the street and ate a hot dog and had some coffee, then caught the train home. He'd told his girlfriend—April!—what had happened and she said now she wanted a hot dog, too. That was the way it used to be.

Audrey and he had just gone here because the accountant was running late and they didn't want to sit alone, together, in a quiet office for 45 minutes.

"No, she was saying that we were a cute couple -"

" - of minutes and we should head back up there, yeah?" Audrey said.

I'd divorce you all over again, thought Ray.

*****

Into the kitchen walked Ray, and the sink was teetering with dishes. They kissed, and Audrey said she was going to hang out in the bedroom for a while. She exited the way he'd come, and he continued to the living room, where their daughter was in front of the television, her eyes glazed, her jaw slack. She didn't look at him as he walked in. He said, "It is time to accompany your father to the park, Tot."

She sighed but dutifully shut off the television which, provided the electric bill was paid, would never hide from her in its room to drink.

At the park, kicking a soccer ball back and forth with his daughter, Ray wondered about the "emotional intimacy" line. That was a good one. Was daylighting the secrets of their relationship to a partial third party cheating? Audrey was such an unreliable narrator in person that his head swam at the thought of what she'd say about him to her friends, who had developed a side-eye game so strong that he wondered what it was he was supposed to have done. Whatever it was, he had no fond memories of it to rely on now.

Was it worse than fucking someone? Let's say, for instance, at that moment the photo was snapped, Ray had said, "My wife is an alcoholic." Would the cheating be one of the flesh (his hands on Tawny's New Boobs) or the lips? Which was worse?

And who was Audrey talking to if that line had made it into the script?

Ray did not see Audrey for the rest of the day. Their parental style had evolved to a place where the two of them were in the same room with their child almost never. As soon as Ray got home from work, Audrey disappeared somewhere. Ray fed her, bathed her, tucked her in, and then Audrey would emerge from the recesses of the house. They'd watch their programs, drink a little, have sex. He knew that most couples at this point in the decay of their marriage didn't even have sex, or had replaced sex with money. But they didn't really have money. It could be worse. He figured he could make it to their daughter's high school graduation this way.

He'd forgotten the afternoon's sinkside monologue when, in the pre-sleep darkness of the bedroom, she said, "Don't you think it's kind of funny that other people are buying houses?"

He jerked alert. Audrey was a keen dramatist and picked fights that started in the middle of the scene so the audience would have to catch up.

"No?" Ray said. "Why would I think - "

"Because this is not the way to live, hand to mouth, meanwhile you come in dripping with judgment about how I raise my kid - "

"- *Our* - "

"And I take care of the kid. And you're not here. And I make lunch. And there's only so much patience that I have. I start the day with a full bucket of patience. Then the bucket is empty. It's empty! It's empty. So of course I put her in front of the TV. Because I can't play pretend games with her all day. I can't! I can't."

"So you're saying you can't?"

(While he didn't love their fights, Ray did find Audrey's Rule of Threes kind of soothing. It allowed him to ruminate for a moment on the type of parent who referred to its offspring as "my kid." There was always something defiantly negligent about such a person. A person you'd expect to say, "Dinner was this Whitman's Sampler box because *you can't tell me how to raise my kid.*" Ray was happy George C. Scott hadn't lived to experience such people, or to hear the expression "break the Internet.")

"...And I can't be cheating on you simply by sharing emotional intimacy with other people." she was saying.

"Yeah!" Ray said, "I was wondering about that! Why did you say that?"

"I can't be cheating on you simply by sharing emotional intimacy with other people," Audrey said.

"You're glitching," Ray said. "It's like I'm bringing an ensemble to your Night of Monologues, Lady MacNugget."

"Fuck you, you fucking failure. Gambler. Racist. Addict. Abuser - "

"*What*?" (Ray totally agreed with "failure," though.) In extremis, Audrey would unload her whole arsenal of projected self-hatred on him, hoping something would stick, and he'd spend so much time batting the more outrageous accusations away ("I'm a school shooter now? *Really*?") that she could at least call him "defensive."

This was what arguments with Audrey were like. At some point she'd begin trying things out in Hartford. Or it was as if Ray had tapped into someone else's game of Missile Command in which missiles were coming from everywhere—from underneath! From behind the game console!—and the cities were well on their way to being leveled.

"And you're tomcatting around - " Audrey said -

" - with my hands full of Tawny's tits," Ray said, exhausted. "See? We finish each other's sentences."

He got up. "I can't stand this," he said. "I'm going to do the dishes." He walked out.

She said something loud enough for him to know she had said something but not loud enough for him to hear.

At the sink he ran the water over his hands until it scalded, then he began washing the dishes.

"Well either you are closing your eyes to a situation you do not wish to acknowledge," he said, after a few minutes, "or you are unaware of the *caliber of disaster* indicated by the presence of a pool table in your community."

CHAPTER XXXIV

DAMN YOU, JOHN

Julia Child's ladle got wedged
In my butt ("Exit Only!"—alleged)
Such haute-French cuisine
Has ne'er been seen
Since the last time the swole Seine was dredged.

CHAPTER XXXV

THE FLIGHT OF THE PINE NUT

HIGH ABOVE THE HARD PATCHWORK of the Mojave Desert Lt. Grimm piloted his tiny, dart-like plane. The sun seemed distant and cold but the earth was farther away than he'd ever been from it; it was as if he could see a curtain parting in the afternoon sky, allowing him access to First Class. He was also about to cut himself off from the only home he knew. The plane flew higher.

The Arrowhead Program was just another of thousands of top-secret experiments, all named by a computer in Princeton, NJ to be indistinguishable to all but the most high-level officials. Still, Arrowhead's importance had been making the rounds about the base for 18 months, and Charlie Grimm felt a quiet thrill when his team leader gave him the assignment. It was to be an exhausting and, truth be told, emotionally wrenching eight weeks of training, Grimm knew, but when would he get such an opportunity again?

And why else was he here?

The new plane was to fly higher than any previous sub-orbital vehicle. It was to "break the surly bonds of earth," etc. and dock with the new Gil Gerard Space Station. The propulsion technology had been around for years, but heat shields sufficient to withstand the re-entry of such a small craft had only become viable very recently. What made Project Arrowhead so exciting was that the plane's debut would be a manned mission. Dudes Not Dogs, as the proud men said in the barracks.

Grimm had said goodbye to his family. His two sons were too young and would not remember him; his wife, Lupita (herself an Air Force brat) choked back tears as she stood on the porch of their home in Nogales. But she knew it was right. The 18-hour training days worked only too well to allow him to forget her.

By that blinding October afternoon when he was strapped into the craft he knew so well, he was not his own man: he was Project Arrowhead's Charlie Grimm.

The earth fell away and darkness beckoned. Others had been higher, but not as naked to the outside. His head was clear, his body relaxed. His training had paid off. Plus, he was the best. He'd known that since high school, since—God, he'd always known it.

That was why it was such a shock to be treated so severely by the aliens. When they came, they kept cooing the most vicious and demeaning things in his ear. Things like, "I'll make you my cow," and "No one ever loved you." The Gil Gerard had been in sight, he had even made radio contact with the cosmonauts therein, when the plane shuddered so violently that he passed out. When he awoke, he was in a room very much like his kitchen, but in his cereal bowl were not Wheaties but genital-free mini-clowns; instead of Lupita standing there in her pajama top drinking orange juice in the morning sun, there was a 30-foot viscous-looking thing covered in tongues and licking a branch-like stick of what appeared to be ice milk. "Wipe it," it said, and it said this Forever, until poor Lt. Grimm's head exploded.

Project Arrowhead was a resounding success. Lupita did not come to the funeral, nor did the two boys. The parents of Charlie Grimm, pensioners living in Florida, were not alerted by the Air Force. To them, Charlie had died in a friendly-fire snafu in Iraq in February, 1991. They had already gone to the closed-casket funeral at Arlington 20 years ago. Lupita, Charlie's high school sweetheart, had cried for about two minutes, then continued behaving unmentionably with Charlie's best friend Ray in the back seat of Charlie's own Vega to the strains of George Harrison's "Wreck of the Hesperus."

Yes, the Arrowhead Project had taken place entirely in Charlie's mind, with microscopic cosmonaut and alien action figures placed there by Uncle Sam himself. The dart-like plane was actually a pine nut; the Mojave Desert, a glistening drop of retsin.

This is why your refund wasn't bigger.

CHAPTER XXXVI

LIFE IN THE MUSKRAT LANE

Through the colitas-fogged past we reveal
That The Eagles stabbed more than their meal
"We called up the Captain
And he got us all tapped in
For a tussle with Toni Tennille."

CHAPTER XXXVII

PHIL AND DON

THE THINGS WHICH MAKE US grieve often involve Shriners, Ray thought. The thought left him cold: 33rd-degree-Mason cold. Ray looked out the window to the street, where Frank was being quartered at the bumpers of departing miniature cars, the result of some remark he'd made about how Catholic burn units stay crispy longer.

Audrey and Bette crossed in the hallway outside, locked in a crablike secret handshake no doubt designed to exclude Ray in particular. It was a tough day. The coffeemaker wept a small sludge into Ray's cup. The rain washed away Frank's remains from the street, but with a monsoon-ish effort; the quartering hadn't been exact, because no Protestant can ever synchronize his acceleration, and for too long Once-Was-Frank lay accusingly on the cobblestones.

Three o'clock. Staff meeting. Frank's chair had been removed, and their three chairs formed a pleasant scalene triangle. An effort was being made, albeit a nocturnal theses-tacking sort of effort, to carry on. Frank hadn't been a good worker; his last three accounts had fallen through due to his negligence, and maybe his violent death would lead to greater efficiency. The accounts were divvied up without mention of their previous caretaker.

I will eat their Calvinist crackers, Ray thought, *I will spread their Calvinist cheese.*

The business was mostly concluded, and Bette closed her briefcase. Audrey and Bette moved to get up. "Wait," Bette said, "I suppose we should talk about Frank."

"I feel uncomfortable," Audrey said, "maybe it's too soon."

"The bylaws require we open things up to discussion and that each non-officer be given time to express feelings and ask questions," Bette said. "Please don't make this difficult for me, gang."

Ray and Audrey looked around the conference table, to the place where Frank once sat. In the corner Ray suddenly spied Frank's old chair, undimpling in the shadows.

"I feel sadness, and hurtness," Ray said. "?"

"Good," Bette said. "That's one for you."

Bette made a little checkmark on a form, then flipped the page. "Audrey?"

"Uh, I think it was John Donne who said that each man's death diminishes him?"

"Attagirl," Bette said. "Let it flow."

One other person said one more thing, but it was inconsequential. Bette watched the second hand move from 10 to 12, smiled, and gently clicked a return key. The group heard an email whiz away.

"Nobody liked Frank," Bette said, "and though his death is an injustice, it serves our purposes. You two are going to split Frank's job and salary between you. The company will save money on his benefits package."

Everything Bette said was absolutely true. Was Frank due some points just for dying? Despite this, it all seemed so cold. Now there was a silence around the table that wasn't OSHA-mandated.

Presently Ray heard heavy, flapping footfalls on the carpet outside, and soft klaxon respiration. And the soft trundling of electric motors and little wheels, up and down the hallway, like an endlessly wandering Danny Torrance, heading for a meeting with the Delbert Grady's daughters that was this room.

Shriner clowns. So it had all been planned.

Still, Ray knew of many companies where extra work didn't mean extra pay. Ray would do anything for money.

"Ah! The men of the hour," Bette said, trundling out a large vat of McDonaldland Orange Drink. "Do me a favor: Open the door."

CHAPTER XXXVIII

POLYGLOT TRAMPSTAMP

Since I'm—above all—"The Cool Dad,"
I'll not "diss" your "ink" as a "fad."
Just please be aware
That tat you've got there
Reads "Long live Islamic Jihad."

CHAPTER XXXIX

PUT: FOR ACTORS UNAFRAID OF THEIR FEELINGS

WE ARE IN A TASTEFUL GOVERNMENT LAB. RAY, in a jonny, is getting ready for a procedure to be performed by DOCTOR AUDREY, who readies her instruments.

DOCTOR AUDREY
You're afraid.

RAY
There are things - in my mind - I hesitate to uncover.

DOCTOR AUDREY
But this is science.

RAY
That's what I tell myself, and I feel better, but only a little. The thing is -

DOCTOR AUDREY
Let's not get into "the thing." Let's not get into what it "is."

RAY
I need to explain.

DOCTOR AUDREY
Let me explain something to you, Fella. We are in a position to crack something open, for science, and you're here telling me about your feelings.

RAY
Yes.

DOCTOR AUDREY
In 1954 there was a study. The government funded a study. Do you know why?

RAY
Um. (?)

DOCTOR AUDREY
Because Necessity directed the government to fund a study, and your government does what is necessary to keep that greedy bitch Necessity puffed up on sweet rolls and chocolate covered cherries, playing with its toes.

-PAUSE-

RAY
I know.

DOCTOR AUDREY
The study sought to quantify the difference between people

who do things for science, and people who do things for feelings, and to find the percentage of people who have feelings about science. What they found, the people doing the study, the people of long ago, some of whom, however, are still alive, was not surprising. What was surprising, ah, Ray, was how much this study cost, in 1954 dollars.

RAY
Does it matter how much the study cost?

DOCTOR AUDREY
Yes. It matters a lot. You see, Ray, the study cost 74 billion dollars, enough to infect every man, woman, and child on the planet with gonorrhea and then cure them, using prostitutes for the first part and vaccine for the second part.

RAY
74 billion dollars could do a lot of things.

DOCTOR AUDREY
Yes, but particularly the thing with the prostitutes. Ray, I developed that plan (we called it Don't Be Afraid To Love Yourself 32X) and I championed it, but Necessity directed the government, ah, otherly. Needless to say, if I was going to get gonorrhea, I was going to have to get it myself, and so would America.

RAY
I can't see how either plan was worthwhile, for science or America.

DOCTOR AUDREY
That's why you're some kind of douchebag, you douchebag.

RAY
Doctor Audrey-

DOCTOR AUDREY
Ray.

RAY
What?

DOCTOR AUDREY
You said my name, so I said yours.

RAY
Oh. Doctor Audrey-

DOCTOR AUDREY
RAY.

RAY
Right. Doctor, I –

DOCTOR AUDREY
Don't, Ray. I can't hear an argument from you. We have gone beyond that point. That point in time. It's time to drill into your head and find what we think is there.

RAY
And if it isn't?

DOCTOR AUDREY
You won't know. You won't *remember*. A *thing*. Where once was a

lobe, there will now be a handle. You will be able to be carried around like a first-generation iMac. Either way that will happen, but if things unfold the way we want them, and we can find that magical liquid that constitutes the under-sheen of your brain, the substance that makes it so shiny - well, we'll be really pleased. Really wicked pleased.

RAY
That substance –

DOCTOR AUDREY
We also call it maize.

RAY
You *do*? That substance, Doctor. Well, I put it there.

DOCTOR AUDREY
You what?

RAY
Yes. You know the lady who runs the MRI machine?

DOCTOR AUDREY
Dee Dee?

RAY
I needed to see her again. I knew there was no good reason. I had to find some way, you see, ah, because I wanted to, ah, have sex with her. So I mixed some Pina Colada Mix and Tang and injected it into my brain.

DOCTOR AUDREY

You fudged the results.

RAY
Well I fudged something, you know what I mean?

(THEY laugh)

That's what gave me my super powers, and why I can set fires from so far away. That's all it is. I needed to see her again. Uh, I can show you. I didn't mean to have it get this big. I just don't want you to cut into my brain. It's Pina Colada Mix and Tang. And I shot it right under my ear.

DOCTOR AUDREY
Wow. That's wonderful.

RAY
Well, yeah.

DOCTOR AUDREY
Hmm.

RAY
So can I go? Dee Dee's outside, and I think she's going to give me her Netflix password.

DOCTOR AUDREY
But we've spent all this money, Ray.

RAY
But Audrey!

RAY just now realizes he's strapped in.

DOCTOR AUDREY
Doctor. All we have is our jobs, Ray.

RAY
But I can show you.

DOCTOR AUDREY
If I let you go, I'll have to let the monkeys go, the gerbils go, the bunnies go. I learned long ago that there's no whores for scientists, Ray. I'm sorry.

RAY
Oh, all right.

DOCTOR AUDREY
Now relax your brain.

RAY
K.

BLACKOUT

CHAPTER XL

KHARTOUM, KHARTOUM

Confined to a Mexican jail
Your horse becomes pensive and frail
He says, "I'll turn gay
If I don't get some hay."
(It's lucky his wife posted bale.)

CHAPTER XLI

EYES OF THE EAGLE

IT WAS A SONG ABOUT AMERICA. It was a song about Freedoms. I heard it playing in the truck as I came back up the driveway with the newspaper. Daddy had her idling and the yard was filled with rich smoke.

"Get in," Daddy said. "Let's play hooky."

I tossed the paper onto the porch. Mama would find it when she came out to feed the chickens.

"No," Daddy said. "Go in there and put it on the kitchen table. Don't make your mother bend over with those heel spurs."

I walked in the house. Mama was there staring at the vinyl tablecloth, chasing some eggs around the plate with a soggy piece of bread. AM radio played traffic on the sevens. I placed the paper by her coffee. She didn't look at it.

"Guess I'm going out with Daddy today," I said.

"I know," she said.

Something about healthcare and troop surges and Russia on the front page. I wiped my fingers on my sweatshirt where they left inky streaks. It was an omen to those who could read the signs: colors ran when unalienable rights were being abridged.

The truck was cold despite the cloud of exhaust it sat in. The vinyl bench seat was blue and cracked. Daddy put her in gear and we bumped down the road. Since there were no seat belts, our upper bodies often touched when he swung wide, with our legs remaining stationary like some Hayes Code couple. I watched the vapor from our breathing fill the frigid cab.

"There's something that you oughtta know," he said. I let it hang. I wasn't going to say "OH WHAT IS IT?" and make a fool of myself. He'd taught me that somehow.

He wasn't going to tell me they were getting a divorce, that he'd decided to pay for college, that it was time for me to go back to church. We passed the tobacco fields in silence, the sun glinting off the dew, a lone cormorant in the distance. He opened his Thermos—a real Thermos—and poured me a cup of straight black sludge.

"Mama's best diesel fuel brew," he said, not taking any for himself.

"Daddy - " I said.

"Now you shut up a goddamn minute," he said.

That was something, right there. That old violence. It took me a moment to realize that what I felt was comfort. He hadn't hit me in years. One day he'd just looked at me, mid-swing, and declared, "What's the point?"

It hadn't been me getting too big and laying him out, it hadn't been some epiphany that corporal punishment never solved anything and that it was counterproductive for children to fear their parents. It was his practical understanding that violence, also, wasn't going to get through to me.

Now he was telling me to shut up like he still felt we had something to say to each other. However many things our fathers are—thoughtful, wise, loving, kind, patient—they'd lose their potency if we didn't sense some menace now and then. I settled back in the chair and listened.

In the morning sun I saw it all. The white stubble, the slight squint of blue eyes as we headed east, his cap pulled low. There was a faint bruising on his cheek, an old man's stain, something that could have happened—at his age—from the simple act of landing on the pillow wrong. The indignity. He looked right as he steered left, glancing at me as we pulled out onto Pinchworm Boulevard. Just a gentle alighting of his eyes on me, the smallest acknowledgment, and then we were out of the intersection and he was looking straight ahead again.

And yet that small stolen glance was so intimate and unexpected. When was the last time he'd looked me in the eye? Fear came rumbling from my innards.

"Look at this town with the factory shut down," he said, "from jobs that they sent overseas."

I turned my head to the right. We were climbing Prospect Hill, and I could see clear across the Valley to Signal Hill. Both sides of the river were vivid in the red brick mill buildings, now converted to factory warehouses, artists' lofts for really bad artists, the only legal pornographers outside of California, and not much else. It was a strangely beautiful -

"When's the last time you saw Signal Hill from here?" he barked.

"Never," I said. It had come to me: the vinyl mill, the plasticworks, the leatherette processor, the rendery, and the bricksmith had all happily belched near-solid waste into the sky for as long as I remembered. Now that was all gone. The air was clean but there was no one down there to breathe it.

"All gone," he said. The truck scaled the road in silence until we stopped at the ruins.

It was nature's wonder how quickly Daddy's workplace of three decades had been reclaimed by the mountain. The Vinyl Mill atop Prospect Hill had been a showpiece of industrial design for its time, but armies of derelicts, no-good kids, and feckless condo developers could not have wrought the destruction simple disuse had. If buildings have souls, the Vinyl Mill had simply given up its own when the place shut down in 1990, its last function a rush re-pressing of "As Nasty As They Wanna Be." The parapets were choked with vines, the moat alive with pumpkins. Birds roosted in the portcullis and deer could be seen through the windows.

My father was crying and Man, it would have been less wrenching if he'd hit me.

I couldn't hold him, couldn't comfort him. We had developed no vocabulary for that. So I stared at his hands, which I regretted even as I couldn't look away. They were massive but papery, like dead wasps' nests. The old gold wedding ring looked heavy enough to pin his left hand to his thigh. When he lifted his mottled mitt and laid it on my shoulder, I felt like the radiologist had clapped an X-ray jacket over me.

"Son, look around at These United States," he said.

"OK," I said.

"Don't let Our Way of Life die," he said. "Son."

"I'll try not to," I said.

"Don't."

We fell silent. The wind rattled the truck in the cold sun.

I can't remember when we'd been close. I was shown pictures from when I was young—*evidence*, my mother said—but I don't remember anything about the days when they were taken. I guess it really went south when I got to school. Back when I was 15, 16, we'd got in some falling down fights. My hair was as long as my mouth was big. One day he'd pulled my hair with all the savagery of a wife beater.

"How does that feel, Cave Bride?" he said. "What if I drag you by your sissy hair down to Valentine's and let them hear you talk about foreigners' rights?"

He added: "Eating all our government's cheese?"

And yet now he sat there, staring at the old Mill, mouth slack, hand twitching on my shoulder. We both felt robbed of something that had never really been ours.

The radio played:

In the eyes of the Eagle
Each man takes his part

From Scottsdale to the Mississippi sun.
These God-given Freedoms
Protect with your heart:
Don't tread on These Colors Don't Run.

I had to open the door because the air in the cab was stifling. I got out and crossed the front of the truck to his side. I watched his eyes track me, but half a step late. It's like he was -

Oh, that was it. Daddy was sick. He was sick. I reached his door and opened it. Some foulness piped out of his side, and he sort of fell into my arms, half out of the door.

"Daddy," I said.

"I loved this country the best that I could," he said.

"Daddy."

"And I loved you, too, Gary," he said. "Just so you know."

His weight was like a bag of straws. Cinnamon sticks. A Santa's bundle full of emaciated refugees that you couldn't believe had lasted this long.

Then he died. His body just got heavier. I struggled to push him back in the cab, where I knew if I at least shut the engine off his body would keep until the coroner came. I didn't drive—another reason for his historical revulsion—so I walked home. I found my mother in the kitchen. She'd switched cigarettes and sections of the paper.

"It's over," I said.

"I'm so sorry, Leon," she said. "It's like the song says: 'My Seven Bizzos.'"

CHAPTER XLII

BROVIDS BEFORE COVIDS

The tyrants mandate that we mask
Our American faceholes. To bask
In the Spray
Of Our Freedoms, I say
Is each Christ-loving Patriot's task.

CHAPTER XLIII

AERIALS

THEY ALL LOOKED SO HEALTHY, Ray thought, even way up here in the thin air. No coffee, no chips—he had lost a dozen pounds—and no devices to hide the world behind save for here and there a pair of glasses.

"You guys," Ray said, speech pressured, unsure of himself, "You guys are fucking serene."

Eight kindly pairs of eyes regarded him. He knew that if it had been a board meeting in front of Bette, Audrey, and Frank that he would have blown it already. But up here on the mountain it was like they thought him a precious child who would grow up in his own blessed time. No rush.

"Just so goddamn serene," Ray said, his voice falling, unable to help himself.

Across the cool yurt/dojo/whatever Yoshi walked, seeming to push no air from him as he did so. Soundlessly he brought Ray a set of flimsy iPod headphones tangled around a set of keys.

"These are the keys from your pocket, and the headphones from your Flash Drive mp3 player," said Yoshi, living in the moment because the previous paragraph is an illusion. "Disentangle them while reciting your koan."

Ray didn't know how his headphones always got so twisted. If asked, he would have told an interviewer that he gracefully folded the wires in a ziggurat pattern, like rich, slow-motion nougat from a candy bar commercial, so there should be none of this tangling like what always engulfed his keys, his gum, his lighter, his pens, his gas receipt, his parking tickets, his life. In went the headphones, out came a pocketful of stuff gathered in the tightest of headphone wires, dense like a star ready to go supernova.

He poked some thumbs into the maze and recited:

"If it's too loud to hear your heartbeat, you're dying. If it's too quiet, you're dead."

He said this until it made all of the sense and none of the sense. When he stopped, his keys were free. He handed both headphones and keys to Yoshi, who handed them to Sara, a 60-year-old woman who mostly poked the earth with her spade, as nothing really grew up here.

That night they all made dinner together, using the same wooden bowl for each course. Everyone's breath smelled, including Ray's. But each had bright, dancing eyes.

After a month on the mountain, Ray greeted each fellow seeker with love. He noted how each of them had at least twice paired off with Sara, the compound's only female.

Afterward the men would retreat somewhere and write songs or poetry. Ray guessed he wasn't at that level of enlightenment yet.

One moment Yoshi appeared in Ray's tent, and told him it was time to go.

"But I just got here," Ray said. "I'm not ready. I still have so much to learn."

Yoshi bade Ray gaze at the valley. Ray slipped on his sandals and accompanied Yoshi to the edge of the mountain. Below they could see skyscrapers. Ray didn't remember this view.

"It is because you've been here 43 years," Yoshi said.

Ray saw. In his left hand were the headphones, now useless, missing one earpiece, but straight and graceful. In his right hand were his keys. Doubtful the car would start now.

"I'll just get my stuff," said Ray, and returned a moment later, because he only had that one System Of A Down CD.

"Not really sure how I'm supposed to return to the world," Ray said to Yoshi, who just nodded, as if to say "I hear what you are saying." Ray thought detachment was a copout.

Half out of camp he spotted Sara, picking berries by the road.

"So today's the day?" she said.

"Yup," Ray said, already distracted. "I think I remember this road. Well, Bye."

"Ray," Sara said, catching up. "I wanted to let you know that I'm bummed we didn't get together. I felt like I'd made my intentions clear to you for most of your 43 years here."

"Yeah, but I was busy," he said. He suddenly wanted a root beer so bad.

CHAPTER XLIV

WELL-REGULATED

From the outhouse our thought leader beckoned
And commanded our bowels be fecund
"It's the Patriot who
Reveres Number Two.
And his favorite Amendment? The Second."

CHAPTER XLV

FEARFUL SYMMETRY

You think that the firmament's flawed
And need constant proof of a God?
Well, it can't just be chance
That, somewhere in France,
There's a guy with ten cats who's named Claude.

CHAPTER XLVI

CASTING THE FIRST STROKE

FOUR DECADES AFTER "SHE WALKED IN THROUGH THE OUT DOOR (OUT DOOR)," the woman wearing the title garment of Prince's 1985 song "Raspberry Beret" continues to puzzle and intrigue scholars.

THE HABERDASHERY-FRAMBOISE OF PRINCE

But it is the narrator who has emerged as a dangerous and unstable sociopath.

"I was working part-time in a five-and-dime," the narrator begins, telling us that his employer, a Mr. McGee, had to repeatedly tell him that the narrator's "leisurely" attitude toward work engendered feelings of dislike in his employer for not only the narrator but also the narrator's social, ethnic, racial, political, or religious group, i.e. "kind."

People with developmental disorders often need to be told several times to complete tasks such as those required in the type of retail establishments where the learning-disabled may find work.

We introduce the notion of the narrator's own mental impairment as the basis for his attraction to the beret-wearing girl. While there is anecdotal evidence to suggest that "opposites attract," it is more often the case that interpersonal relationships are founded on shared values and interests.

If the narrator is autistic, however, he is high-functioning, as demonstrated by his ability to vary his menial tasks in order to hold his own interest:

"It seems that I was busy doing something close to nothing," he says, as if observing someone else, "but different than the day before."

It is then that he sees the subject of the song, as "she walked in through the out door." Consistent with Persistent Developmental Disorder (Not Otherwise Specified), he repeats "out door."

"She wore a raspberry beret," he tells us, "The kind you'd find in a second hand store."

Researchers disagree on whether the narrator's choice to speculate where the girl might have found her beret is Asperger's Syndrome-style "Information Bombardment" or a genuine attempt to connect with the listener.

In any case, and appearing to validate PDD-NOS theorists, he compulsively, almost fetishistically repeats her headwear throughout the song, adding that, were the temperature appropriate, the probable group home resident might not "wear much more."

Up to this point in the interview, academics have been inclined to agree that the narrator, whether a stroke or head trauma victim or otherwise mentally compromised, was basically an amiable and harmless person, even if he might have proven a minor management problem to his employer.

But alarm bells sound in the next set of lyrics.

The narrator, based on the girl's inappropriate entrance to the five-and-dime as well as her hat (and his opinions about whether or not she would wear nothing but the hat should the weather become "warm"), makes a compulsive and staggering logical leap:

"I think I love her," he says.

While condemnation of the narrator's premature profession of love is unanimous in university and medical circles, the following lines divide scholars:

"Built like she was, she had the nerve to ask me if I planned to do her any harm," he says.

Does this mean she was attractive to the narrator and, knowing this, that she would disregard a reasonable person's fear of being harmed by him?

Or was she unattractive to the narrator ("Built like she was, she had the nerve to ask me...") and therefore unworthy of questioning his malicious intent?

Either way, it is clear that she recognized the danger; when does it come up unless someone is in danger the question of whether they are to be harmed?

The American Psychiatric Association recommends a simple Appropriateness Test, which it calls the Cocktail Metric:

"Go to a cocktail party and approach a friendly-seeming stranger with the statement in question," its literature suggests. Would you approach an amiable stranger and ask them if they planned to do you any harm?

It gets worse:

"So look here, " the narrator challenges us, "I put her on the back of my bike and, uh, we went riding down by Old Man Johnson's farm."

Not "she got on the bike willingly and of her own volition" but "I put her on the back of my bike" like a wounded or trophy animal. Perhaps due to abuse, trauma, or the schizoid belief that he is a being that draws power from celestial bodies, the narrator then observes that his ability to perform sexually is influenced by the visibility of the sun or the moon.

"Overcast days never turned me on," he says, and then for the first time openly derides the girl by comparing her to noxious smog:

"But something about the clouds and her mixed."

The narrator then savagely beats the girl with his feet, attempting to make the listener believe that she was not only the aggressor but also that she wanted him to beat her with his feet.

"She wasn't too bright, but I could tell when she kissed me," he says, " – she knew how to get her kicks."

Having dragged her into some kind of stable, silo, or manger, the narrator feels an almost lycanthropic connection to nature.

"Rain sounds so cool when it hits the barn roof," he says, and researchers concede that he's right: Rain does sound cool that way. But we shouldn't let the sociopath charm us with his studied behaviors of normal human interaction.

Because then, as if denying his own humanity (and the responsibility of his crime) by attributing human characteristics to animals, he attempts to divert listeners' attention to his temporary stablemates.

"...And the horses wonder who you are."

As if shaking his fist at a universe only half-complicit in his offenses, the narrator goes on to accuses Nature that "thunder drowns out what the lightning sees (and) you feel like a movie star," (possibly Hannibal Lecter, the Son of Sam, Leatherface from "The Texas Chainsaw Massacre," or even Satan, as depicted in several films).

The narrator invokes this pandemonium of murderers as "They": "They say the first time ain't the greatest," he says.

Boldly addressing us again and bragging of his lack of remorse: "But I'll tell you, if I had the chance to do it all again, I wouldn't change a stroke."

The narrator's megalomania at its zenith, he taunts listeners by referring to them collectively as an infant, hinting that the girl is no longer alive:

"Baby, I'm the most," he says, "with a girl as fine as she was then."

I'm comforted that Prince acknowledged that "Raspberry Beret" was about ex-girlfriend Susan Moonsie and that reliable documentation exists that Moonsie's intelligence fell within normal limits. Furthermore, despite the repeated shellacking Prince's bands dealt to outfits led by Morris Day, or his baptist-like fervor in dumping women into Lake Minnetonka, the late Prince himself was not criminally insane.

I'm hoping to use this abstract to get my Ph.D. in Depth Psychology and become either a Licensed Marriage & Family Therapist or realtor in the State of California. Wish me luck! And remember: unless we're talking about Shadowfax of the Mearas or Brego of the Rohirrim, horses, like the Cormorant, don't wonder about you at all.

CHAPTER XLVII

WHAT DOES BRAINTREE EVEN MEAN?

In re: restricting the vote
Abigail Adams once wrote
"John, it's just more fake news
That Ladies can't choose—
I'll give you one term in the scrote."

CHAPTER XLVIII

WHAT DIDN'T HAPPEN

HE KNEW WHY HE'D SAID IT: he'd thought it was funny. But remorse set in, as it did for Ray, quickly, on little cat feet, and smelling like little cat breath.

Audrey had been inspired the other evening and got out of bed just as the two of them were getting into it (not the bed). She'd said, probably pushing some hair out of her face—though Ray didn't know because it was dark—that she wanted to try something *new*.

"You're going to clean the house?" Ray said, and regretted it immediately, not because Audrey couldn't take a joke, but because the joke sounded like someone else might have said it. For the next 48 hours Ray tried to narrow it down to certain comedians or people in his acquaintance. Finally, he determined that if someone else hadn't already said it, someone famous would say it very, very soon, and imbue it with his special crowd-pleasing style, and Ray would be left nothing.

Perhaps anticipating this, Ray was petrified when Audrey came back into the bedroom.

"Turn over on your stomach," she told him. Ray felt his whole body clench, folds of skin grabbing onto other folds of skin, the way a hamster will carry fistfuls of sawdust with him when you pick him up by his eye. Ray did as he was told because he didn't want to offend her. He wanted to encourage adventuresome behavior. Still, he was scared as hell that she would begin putting things up his ass, the result of some overheard cafeteria conversation or the advice of some sassy overweight friend from Hot Springs he knew she didn't have. First would come a finger, and then a broom handle, and then a taxiing 737 Dreamliner. When would it stop? Soon, so many things would be up his ass that there'd be no room left for him.

But this relationship must go forward, Ray thought, chewing the pillow, so I will make the ultimate sacrifice, despite the fact that that part of him had never even seen direct sunlight, only the reflected kind, like Plato's cave.

But nothing like that happened.

It was something else. Something not horrible at all. Instead, Audrey dumped a canister of Lincoln Logs on his back and methodically built a model of a futuristic YMCA there, using every log.

Audrey's talent was in convincing Ray she'd done this, because there were no mirrors in the room for him to check her work. As the logs depressed him further into the bed, he thought he could really feel the indoor track, the locker room, and the sauna. He could feel the limited parking outside. He could feel neighborhood kids getting a second chance through basketball and boxing. Audrey had done all this.

Audrey kept surprising him, so Ray had to continually update his Audrey database with new fields. Now he could perform additional sorts on Audrey Who Builds Things On My Back and Audrey Who Appears As If She's About To Put Things Up My Ass But Doesn't. Wonderful new things to think about.

Later, he said: "I thought you were going to put things up my ass," and she said: "I never, ever will."

Still, he wondered if she'd ever clean the house.

CHAPTER XLIX

GETTING BACK OUT THERE

Adventures in innocent trysting
Arise from each classified listing
The questions, perforce:
Up mine or up yours?
Revolve around ***three kinds*** *of fisting.*

CHAPTER L

MIDNIGHT AT THE DAMNATION

THIS CASINO WAS DIFFERENT. The discerning gambler could tell from the moment he walked in. It had an atmosphere unlike any in the desert city because the pumped-in oxygen was mixed with rich, creamery butter that left its customers shimmering with a golden glaze, as if they were the gods that had turned their faces from the rest of the establishments on the Strip.

It was a bad time for Damnation's neighbors. The themes had dried out. The Hall of Justice, with its constantly-circling invisible jet (actually it was just Lynda Carter tethered in a seated position, but she'd signed the contract) and its 400-foot crouching Space Monkey, Gleek, only attracted certain low-income slacker-led families and, kitty-corner across the street, Andersonville's daily Civil War re-enactments left the heretofore immaculate Vegas gutters running with blood. Gone were the stalwarts Comic Sands, David Bowie's Aladdin Sane, and Midway's Pac-Man casino, all victims of the inevitable Bring Your Kids to Vegas backlash. But Damnation's secret owners were quickly buying up the old properties for its expansion, which was already facilitated by a People Mover, 12 supersonic monorails, a nuclear submarine that navigated through a sea filled with volcano-distilled Icelandic vodka, and a luge stocked with topless gymnasts.

Damnation satisfied the clientele that bemoaned the gradual loss of Vegas' beloved seediness to conventions and the wholesome-ish tourist trade. But it was also family-friendly in that it was the only hotel/casino/entertainment complex that resolutely embodied a narrative and theme, and better than any of its predecessors had. After all, every other casino's theme was borne out exclusively by the décor: the Tokyo's guests walked through Godzilla's legs to get in, the Autobahn's greeters were dressed like Falco (who had just given up being Austrian, and dead), and the Knight Rider's elevators called everyone Michael. But each casino had the same machines, the same stores, and the same squinty, jaundiced blackjack dealers, as if one giant UNICEF package full of roulette wheels and waitresses had fallen in the middle of the Nevada desert and then the buildings had fallen on top of them.

The Damnation's theme was Hell And How to Get There. A 400-story underground complex with its front door and check-in counter in Las Vegas and pentacular side entrances in Los Angeles, Area 51, Banff, Newark, and San Antonio, the Damnation had everything: legal and illegal prostitution, depending on what suited you, 24-hour steak dinners, a transcontinental railroad, four-mile long two-dollar limit craps tables where you had to fire the dice out of a cannon so that they'd bounce off the opposite wall, and nine circles of torment and misery, color-coded for easy access.

Hard-knuckled gangster-types, jaded Hollywood slicksters, and tough-talking femmes-fatale would pass through whichever bolgia appealed to them—Lust, Incontinence, Heresy, whatever—to spend the butter-soaked days and nights gaining the world but losing their souls. Limited-budget seniors and young families alike would take heed of the neatly-packaged debauchery around them while enjoying subterranean roller coasters, special effects-heavy shows like Blow Up Iran, in which Iran is blown up, and, like everyone else, 24-hour steak dinners.

After days of wholesome and not-so-wholesome excess, all comers would be tossed, screaming and terrified, into the fiery pit at the center of the Damnation complex. In its depths their lives would be judged and they would go on to spend eternity in non-cleansing flames.

Naturally, that is why Damnation's one simple billboard, propped cartoonishly in the sand that was once Las Vegas and which now served as Damnation's roof, read: *Inevitable Style.*

CHAPTER LI

IN THE FRAGRANT NATATORIUM

In love with a mermaid? Think twice
And remember this piece of advice:
When she tells you, "Go south,"
Just breathe through your mouth
Because wearing a snorkel's not nice.

CHAPTER LII

SOMETIMES WE EXPLAIN OURSELVES

"'**OUT OF THE BOX' DOESN'T JUST** describe how I eat cereal," said Ray on his first job interview in several years, "but you could say the same thing about where my cats poo and my thinking."

Frank was silent. Ray's old co-worker was now Human Resources Manager at BlimpCorp.edu, kind of an Outward Bound with zeppelins. Frank had assured him the interview was only a formality, but Ray was nervous.

And when he was nervous, he talked too much.

"Not only that," Ray stammered, "but I successfully sued my old employer for wrongful termination, representing myself in court. I maintained scrupulous documentation of every infraction, and even the judge praised how organized I was."

"Boy, I can't see why we wouldn't hire you," said Frank.

Ray's more recent employment history wasn't spotty—he was acknowledged the best in his field. But it was a skillset that was difficult to transfer, much less explain. And he was getting little help from Frank.

"Leon will want to know what you've been up to the past few years," Frank said, tapping Ray's CV. "There's a bit of a *gap*. Were you in the forest somewhere, finding yourself?"

"No, I was just, just —"

Audrey had left a few weeks ago. Ray had just begun shaving again that morning. He hadn't been up this early in a while. Things seemed almost painfully bright. He could hear the electricity in the lights of Frank's office, could see the gelled spikes of Frank's hair, could smell the cologne. For a moment Ray spied a single crumb marring the corner of Frank's lower lip and, as if signaled, Frank whipped out a handkerchief and gently daubed the crumb away. He fed the handkerchief like a bank deposit into a hidden slot in his desk, and Ray could hear the tiny, whirring motor that accepted that handkerchief and who knows how many others into the recesses of Frank's desk and, perhaps, the Blimp-Corp Personal Linen Services beyond.

"Just what?" Frank demanded, edging forward in his seat. Ray remembered that Frank had been very competitive, but hadn't the past decade changed all their lives? Wasn't it reasonable to assume Frank wasn't interested in beating Ray anymore?

"Just that I'd prefer not to mention what I've been up to," Ray said. "People always give me funny looks."

"I heard somewhere that you were a juicer," Frank said, the slightest smile on his face.

"Juicer" was Audrey's word. Ray might have known Frank would be one of the stops on her post-Ray circuit.

"Yes," Ray said. "A lot of people will buy a machine to juice their fruits and vegetables, but I exorb them by hand. I built up a very impressive clientele, and by the end I was juicing for everybody."

"*Artisanal*," mused Frank, barely able to contain himself.

"Yes, God Damn It, Artisanal," Ray declared. "I was an artisanal juicer. And I could wring fluid from anything. People were bringing their kids to me to drain their ears."

"I'm sure that was very satisfying work," Frank said. "Kids lying around the waiting room in a heap with the beets and the carrots and melons. Certainly seems satisfying and a, um, personal triumph..."

Frank trailed off but quickly composed himself, folding his hands on the desk and looking at Ray as if the conversation were over and there were things to do.

"Do I get the job or not?' Ray said.

"Oh, I'll pass this CV along to Leon," Frank said, standing up smartly and guiding Ray to the door. "But I'm not sure how such a hands-on kind of person like yourself will fare in a theory-driven company like this one."

"Exorption isn't all I do," murmured Ray. "Nobody does just one thing anymore."

"Should have thought of that before you made these business cards," Frank said, expertly flicking Ray's "Exorption Is All I Do" card from his front pocket. Triumphant.

"You always hated me."

"Yet here you are," Frank said.

CHAPTER LIII

EASY ON THE SYRUP, WALTER

The shrieks from the basement remind
My children to always be kind
And fear ***GOD****, for they know*
That their sister below
Forgot to say grace when she dined.

CHAPTER LIV

LADY AND THE MAN

SOMETIMES you'd see them hanging off each other, sobbing. These places made me uncomfortable. I'd sit in the scattershot grouping of chairs and watch them dance. They looked like heavy drapes in a breeze; two people holding each other up, crying for different reasons over their partner's shoulder.

The freedom fighters would say anything to get Wandy's attention. They'd loiter at the Dime A Dance and she'd listen to each one. All their fucked up stories. On their way through *El Pueblo de Nuestra Senora la Reina de Los Angeles de Porciuncula* they'd stop in and look for her. If she wasn't there, they'd march off to install or depose some moustaches-twirling warlord. Republics rose and fell when she was off having those root canals.

When she was there, sitting primly on a stool with a small cushion, her skirts arrayed around her, her flawless olive neck bearing a regal head, they would crowd her like puppies, almost crawling over each other with hopes of getting closer.

"Lady," one would say, "such fruits I will bring you when I return victorious from *Dolor de Cabeza*. Such fruits!"

"My dying wife has given me permission to court you, sweet long-legged Lady," another would say, tears in his eyes, clutching cash. "Say that you will come to *Juenilla* with me."

"I am so lonely," they might all have said. "We will walk into bullets to feel you against us when the music ends."

She would nod to this one or that one, and the man would reach up to hook little brown hands over her sturdy shoulders. She would guide him onto the dance floor like those inexplicable canine companions of blind dogs, nosing its friend to the water bowl. The man would inhale Wandy's perfume like he was trying to snort a room full of gardenias, his eyes closing, birthing tears. Invariably, as the song faded away, he would lose what dignity he'd somehow held onto, and attempt to climb her like a tiny swart mountaineer. She would gently brush him away with a secret squeeze.

They brought her gifts. *Oros de Congrejo*, scented turtles, Thomas Guides with extra pages, secret grids. She took these things, considered them, brooded on them, quietly regifted them when the men departed.

Dancing, the other couples were lost in sadness, orbiting like Plutos about to be stripped of planethood.

But I wasn't lost. I was the DJ. Wandy would slide a crisply-folded fifty into my booth every night to make sure I cut off the songs at 2:30. I'd start the fade at around 1:55 and just slowly turn the knob counter-clockwise. If I were flying a plane, you'd be above the clouds before you even knew you were in the air, I was so smooth.

I paid attention to them all, but mostly to Wandy. She was so tall that her men couldn't tell she wasn't looking at them. She'd focus just past their heads, at her hands clasped behind their necks, at an amulet on a pendant she held between her fingers.

Some nights, when it was slow, I would dance with her to the plaintive rhythms of "Tusk." I was always proud that she looked me in the eye.

"I would like to make sweet love to you, Leon," she said. "By the turgid Tampiquena Sea."

I would lean into her, closing my eyes. But it wasn't to accept the inevitable kiss, just to absorb her sobs. They always came.

"But you cannot catch The Cormorant, can you?" she'd say, and then, to herself: "It's only when I'm dancing that I'm free."

Fleetwood Mac would be walking off USC's field by this point, the whole of the Trojan color guard wondering what the fuck had just happened.

I wasn't going to be the one.

But I knew who it was, and that little bit of Wandy letting me in would have to be enough.

He had come in one night a few years ago. There was unrest over the border. A lot of guys were coming through. In pickups, on donkeys, on these motorized bikes that you can only get in the International Poor People's Catalog. He was a head taller than the rest of them, and he walked in, hatless, full black mane, a little grey at the temples, thin moustache. He looked straight at Wandy and they were on the dance floor before I could even cue up the next song. Silver dimes seemed to sweat from his shiny pants, and the floor soon glistened like the bottom of a mall fountain.

I played the song all the way through, and two more. The other ladies were outraged, their dance partners overjoyed. I played all seven minutes and five seconds of "Light My Fire." I think several men had accidents. Wandy and The Man kept dancing.

Then he gravely produced the pendant from beneath one of his epaulets, clasping it behind her neck. The amulet fell between her breasts, bouncing off each one before it rested, and she blushed. He nodded to her, then walked away. She stood there, swaying, as I played a Dokken power ballad by mistake. She never saw him again.

I guess there must be millions of stories like this, of these unattainable women in port-town bars. Every other week or so I would bring Wandy some sweet white wine or spices from the East (Bellflower, usually, or sometimes Covina), but I never entertained a hope that one night she'd leave with me.

Instead I felt like I was tending to a flame. I didn't want to see that flame go out, even if it didn't burn for me.

One rainy Friday a letter came. It was dirty and rumpled, but it had impressive seals, and Easter Seals stamps. Wandy read it and made to leave, but she only got as far as the dance floor before she crumpled in her skirts, looking so achingly beautiful that I felt my heart would break.

"He has been eaten by ants," she said. "The ants have carried him away."

Two of the younger girls tried to comfort her, but Wandy grew rigid at their approach. The older ladies kept their distance, nursing sadnesses of their own. Surely even Wandy could not withstand the death of her love, they thought. What hope is there for us?

But what this lady did next surprised us like a clickbait headline: she strode to the doors and threw them open. Little men shuffled in, surprised the place opened early, still clutching their outside beers.

That day Wandy danced with all of them to "Kashmir." I was forbidden to touch the faders. Her final three partners got the whole "Houses of the Holy" album.

She was exhausted by the end, and I had to help her to her car, but she drove away with a dreamy little smile that I could see reflected in her rearview mirror.

CHAPTER LV

TRADEOFF

With a beak where her vulva should be
My wife avoids intimacy
But the shellfish she scoops
From the sea when she poops
Redeem our sham marriage for me.

CHAPTER LVI

HEDONIST

THE SUNSET WAS AT his disposal in the rearview mirror as Ray fired gasoline through his leased Civic Hybrid. He was where he wanted to be, heading east to a starchy meal in Glendena. The distracting ocean breezes had stopped at the mountains, bouncing off the trees to land on the coyotes, confusing them. Let the coyotes have their sea air, Ray, thought: I'm getting some daiquiris.

Monthly dinners with lesbian postal employees were one of Ray's many extravagances. Today at CVS he'd bought an extra unit of stick deodorant, just to keep in the car. Things were looking up financially, and he could afford it. He smiled as he accelerated around a curve, blowing through a late yellow. He made a guess, stabbing at a big knob where the radio should be. He was right: shallow-cut classic rock filled the air-conditioned cabin.

"Doing alright," attested Sniff 'n' The Tears, and Ray couldn't agree more. "A little driving on a Saturday night."

Ray's solid-color t-shirt was new, and form-fitting. He'd stopped at the Gap earlier, and had a Jamba Juice on the way out. Reconsidering, he'd walked back into the mall halfway to the garage and found a clean restroom. He hadn't known he'd had to shit that bad. Afterward he changed into his new shirt, making sure he removed the vertical strip of Ls stuck to the back.

"*Not this time*," Ray had said, sadder, wiser, victorious.

(His) Honda loved the new blacktop by the construction in his neighborhood, and the golden hour light made the pawn shop, the check-cashing place, and the eyebrow removal outfit look old-world beautiful. He really liked this new lease, and liked that the company was paying for half of it, not including gas and insurance. Tonight it was easy to love Twisty River.

He thought about his dinner companions. Whenever MaryEllen didn't have a girlfriend she was flirty with him, and Ray knew that tonight she was celebrating one of her many Let's Take A Breaks from Kathy. Don't offend a lesbian for a long enough time, Ray knew, and sometimes she comes back.

Tonight would be appetizers and frozen cocktails, and entrees that would taste even better when he reheated the leftovers. No work tomorrow, maybe a Netflix movie after he came home, or maybe he'd bury his face up some PHP debugging while drinking beer. Every option was a good one.

He decided to take the bridge rather than the freeway. This is the reason these roads were created, Ray thought. It was nice enough, and he had enough time, to park for free in a neighborhood and walk rather than pay a valet something stupid to watch the guy place (Ray's) car 30 feet away. Oh, Ray loved the moment he was in, and the next several hours of them looked good, too.

Tomorrow morning he would sleep.

As he approached the bridge, "Driver's Seat" faded out and Manfred Mann's version of "Blinded by the Light" faded in. Deflate. Ray hated this song. The nod to "Chopsticks" in the break was not clever, and he was offended when the band used the word "Mama." The whole song just didn't need ever to have happened, Ray believed. He blindly threw out his right thumb to change the station.

Thus his last words were: "No, *you're* the douche."

Coming around the corner from the opposite direction was a small motorhome, which Ray's Honda knicked just before he lost control. The little car sailed effortlessly over a low fence and free-fell into a deep ravine below the beautiful bridge.

For a moment he thought of the great weekend he'd been having, and considered that whatever fate lay in store was the result of his simply not being able to stand Manfred Mann one moment longer. Near the end, he was comforted in the knowledge that he'd died fighting.

CHAPTER LVII

EGGPLANT PARM WITH THESES

Had Luther's reformative view
Extended a leap year or two
He'd see that the clowns
From the sub shop downtown
Tack shit up in my lobby, too.

CHAPTER LVIII

HEAD

THE ARRANGEMENT BETWEEN my brother and me is straightforward: neither of us will mention the horrible events of my twelfth birthday and, therefore, we will be allowed to live our lives the way they should be lived—quietly.

I am 46 and Tim is 50. The first day of my sixteenth year began with a snowball fight in the field behind our house in Anola, just outside Winnipeg. It was vicious, like most of the interactions between us. We'd pack the snowballs with ice or rocks or frozen pieces of compost, if available, and let fly. I wasn't bigger than Tim or especially strong, so there was no reason he shouldn't have gone lighter on me.

It seemed like school was always out that winter and, I'm sad to say (now that I'm a parent), our mother was happier not knowing what we were up to. There were some awful things that happened in those woods when I was a kid—an abduction, a murder, rapes. Little grottoes with broken beer bottles and dirty magazines and waterlogged mattresses. Just a kilometer up the trail from our place. Yet Mother would get real antsy if the two of us were in the house too long, so she sent us outside.

You could feel the cold coming up from the wood of your bedroom floor. I'd realize that I was cold gradually because, as I slept, I would pull the covers over my face. Removing the blankets when the sun came up sent a wall of cold air down on me. I guess I needed less air when sleeping. The bright sun through the bare trees, and the cold in the house. Turning on the heat was a luxury. I made a game of walking through the fog of my breath, down to a kitchen of cereal bowls and not enough milk. Tim and I would fight over the Apple Jacks.

There was a seriousness and a structure with which my brother and I beat each other. We were not like well-bred rich kids playing touch football on the lawn; we would set out to draw blood every day. Father worked a lot, but we would see him on Saturday afternoons. By the time we were in our teens, we both dwarfed Father. Still, he could take us down in about two seconds if he needed to make a point, which wasn't often. I describe our fear of him as good-natured.

The day I turned 12, Mother went out in the morning to get my birthday cake. Tim was left in charge, which always rattled me because he had no business telling me what to do. We went outside and began pounding the ice on the pond with sticks. It was frozen to the very edge, so the fun drained quickly. Then we tried to knock the trees down. Sometimes the smaller trees, being frozen, would break if you punched them with your heavy gloves (that was my favorite part about the winter—-you felt invincible in layers). When we tired of that we began punching each other in earnest.

I used to think that if I ever had kids I'd know where they were coming from, because I had what I like to think of as the quintessential childhood: a little hungry, a little bruised, a little mischievous, but generally respectful of my elders and not too put-upon. That said, I don't even know the person I call my daughter. She is like some five-foot-tall exotic pet that scares me silly. Dumb as we were, my brother Tim and I knew we were kids and knew we were doing childish things by beating each other up and throwing ice snowballs at each other. On my twelfth birthday everything changed.

After Tim had punched through a sapling with his bare hands, he put together a snowball packed with ice, deer crap, and a stick. When everything got quiet I became nervous, and turned to see Tim creeping up on me. I saw the uber-ball in his hand and quailed. "Don't you dare," I said.

“This isn’t meant for you,” Tim said. “I saw a fox.”

“No you didn’t.”

“Just keep walking.”

I knew he was lying and that he was angry that I'd turned around when his arm wasn't even half-cocked. For the next fifteen minutes I resigned myself to the fact that I would be smashed in the back of the head with a snowball crammed with special features.

Childhood was painful: much more painful than adulthood has been. Seriously, thinking about your own mortality is a piece of cake compared to going into class the day after Bridget Monahan refused to go out with you. The snowball smashed into the back of my head with a deadly earnest. It's hard to explain now, but though my brother meant to hurt me, it wasn't through a lack of good will. Unfortunately, my brother's snowball went a little too far.

The snowball took off my head. One moment I was studying some bird tracks and the next my head, and therefore my eyes, were flying into the snow. It was a very dense snowball.

Tim's guilt, combined with his unconventional notions of fair play, conspired to make him fish my head out of the snowbank and grind it back onto my neck, which promptly rejected it. Somehow, my arms knew to pick up my head and carry it back to the house, where my no-nonsense but thrice-aggrieved mother sewed my head back on with her best thread. Needless to say, my little sister's potato costume looked pretty ratty that Harvest Faire, with a lot of cheap yarn securing the eye.

Tim almost killed his only brother, and I was almost killed by my only brother. What would have happened if he'd killed me? I know that Tim still fears some long-dormant vengeance. I know that my wife, Rhondat, wonders when I'll finally ask for that raise, demand that raise. She doesn't know that I'm just happy to be alive.

CHAPTER LIX

THE AWAKENING OF MARY INGALLS

I hope that the HVAC guy's late
To this fetid apartment I hate
The more humid, why then it'll
Smell ten times more genital
And I seek to impress my blind date.

CHAPTER LX

DRY

THE PROCEDURE left Ray feeling groggy and—a hospital term—*logy*. All that which had been open was now bound, and Ray was like a ripe peach, delicately seamed around 80 percent of his body, so that he'd never have to expel anything again, except for a bit of unpleasantness once every other week when a woman from the Twisty River Visiting Nurses' Association would come and, catcher's mitt in hand, field an explosive and centralized volley of everything Ray's body could muster up, shot from a tube the size of the one sticking out of your garden-variety Phantasm Ball.

It was to be a contented time for Ray, with no more secretions. The baser things were out of the picture, of course, but there would also be no more sweating, no more salivating, and, most important, no more tears. Feeling head and shoulders above the rest of the world's clowns, Ray looked forward to a time when indeed the world would come around to fulfilling another of Johnson & Johnson's dreams and become Ouchless, too.

But adjusting to his new arid, extra-dry self would prove difficult. Never a peeler, Ray couldn't summon up anything with which to moisten non-peel stamps, so he employed a local lolling sensualist to handle his work correspondence. The gypsy warlock man would lie about on throw pillows, lippily consuming bon bons and sweetmeats, and tongue first more than twice the length of an envelope's lickable area and then, after lapping up some heavy designer half and half, lick the living shit out of all Ray's 68-cent stamps.

There was also the problem of The Ladies. Would the resurgent Audrey be able to cope with his chalkboard eraser puffs of passion or would she gravitate to the more spongiform Frank, always there to trail moisture wherever he went? Ray knew that his would be a ship of the desert-type of existence, and he was feeling especially Sharif-y when Bette walked in.

"I like the salt-flats thing," she said, opening her folders, "you hoping for someone to break a land speed record on you?"

"Oh," said Ray, suddenly flush with nowhere to go, "it's like a new haircut—I'm just trying it out." But he knew the Army Corps of Engineers would have to divert a river through his colon to ever get him damp again. Just then Audrey walked in and it all clicked.

She was as shriveled as a sporting goods store trail mix apricot. The humidity in the air fled from her and coated the walls instead. She walked to the conference table with an audible rustle, settled into her chair like a toothpick through some wedding reception spanikopita, and beamed something from her phone into space, where the digits landed on some dusty planet. She was so dry she could have lathered herself up with some beef jerky. Everything Ray was, Audrey had become, but twice as much.

Could it ever work?

"The Hendertson fiasco," began Bette, and stopped.

Something had happened to Audrey. The morning sunlight, catching motes in the air, also caught Audrey, who swayed like a dormant, desiccated, her-shaped hive. Why was it always bees with that woman?

The office workers were taking Audrey away with rakes and garden implements, shaping her into a pyramid of herself in the corner. Ray could see her smiling.

CHAPTER LXI

SUGARLOAF

Her plan on its face seemed quite brilliant:
Pre-birth, get the egress Brazilian't
But with no hair on board
The tot shot 'cross the ward
— Thank GOD kids today are resilient.

CHAPTER LXII

JAVIER CULO

THE COCA COLA TRUCK RUMBLED into the dry parking lot. Skinny, dusty children helped the man unload three cases into the refrigerator. "I can't keep coming all the way out here for just three cases," the man said to Javier Culo. Javier Culo watched as the man got back in the truck and drove away. It was several squinting minutes in the sun before the truck disappeared past the hill.

The Cokes were still warm when Javier took one from the fridge. Busted. He had to search again today. It was important.

30 years had passed since the red-haired man had stolen Javier's candy cane. Javier himself had been a skinny, dusty child then, but to look at him now one would assume that more than 50 years had passed. Time had been unkind, and Javier Culo had been unkind to himself. He had devoted his life and his sanity to finding the red-haired man, and now there was new information.

What would he do when he found the man? Oh, he knew. He told everybody: "I will hold his neck like I am either strangling a guitar or a chicken. Only on that day shall I decide which. I will wait until he recognizes me. Then I will squeeze and watch the life drain from him."

Did the punishment fit the crime? No. Not even in zero gravity and with compounded interest. But punishments very rarely fit crimes. Javier Culo would make sure the red-haired man never made a child cry again.

It is necessary to mention that, when his candy cane was stolen, Javier himself did not cry. His *madre* asked him *horas* later, when he returned to the sunny *cocina* where the *radio* was playing Taco's remake of "Puttin' on the Ritz," where his candy cane was. "*Donde esta tu candy cane?*" she asked, neglecting the first upside-down question mark because she was illiterate.

"*Ay de mi! El hombre rojo del pelo!*" cried Javier Culo, and with that a vengeance that spanned three decades was born. To be truthful, Javier Culo only swore a lifetime of vengeance because he had a Spanish test the next day for which he hadn't studied. But as is so often the case with needless sprees of violence—or anything not really well-thought out—the justifications came later.

The red-haired man, whose name was Dusty, had spent the last 30 years oblivious to his grave danger at the hands of the madman Javier Culo. But his luck was about to run out.

The two men, joined by fate but separated by years, had been in the same laundromat the day before. Both lived in the same town, *Pierna del Conejito*, in the same neighborhood. But Dusty's woman, Roz, had put her boot through their washing machine in a Zima frenzy and Dusty found himself wrestling Javier Culo for the last packet of Dreft. The two men struggled blindly.

Upon mastering his determined detergental foe, Dusty remarked to the laundry lady, Snizzita, "Just like taking candy from a baby. And I should know—I did it for the American Dental Association for years."

Dusty had been a CC Rider of sorts for the ADA south of the border. His job was to save the teeth of children by limiting access to sweets.

Dusty happened to glance back at the weeping Javier Culo, who met his eyes while scrabbling under the dryer for some fabric softener bits.

So now the journey was over. Javier Culo stopped by the gas station out by the highway. He drank a warm Coca Cola. He reflected on the path his life had taken. That took about two minutes, and then he followed Dusty home. Roz was still in a state, and Dusty went outside to smoke. Javier Culo was waiting. He moved swiftly across Dusty's dirt lot, thumbs out.

"Oh - " Dusty said, another man's hands closing around his neck. He saw the kid from the laundromat. He thought, "*This* punishment sure doesn't fit the crime! - " and then listened as Javier Culo spoke the following, long-rehearsed words:

"Now I have you. You are in my clutches. You shan't escape. I say: You shan't. Do you recognize me?"

"From the laundromat?" Dusty squeaked.

"No," Javier Culo replied, "from long ago. You stole my candy cane."

"No I didn't," Dusty replied, suffocating and confused. "When?"

"30 years ago. In my back yard around the corner."

"Nope. I sure don't recognize you."

"But I am wearing the exact same clothes," Javier Culo cried.

"Is your hair different?"

"No! My hair is exactly the same!"

Swarms of multi-colored bugs began to swim in front of Dusty's eyes. He didn't get it. He was trying to accommodate this fellow, who was so obviously trying to kill him.

"Was there a little girl who lived around the corner?"

"*There were no little girls in my neighborhood!*" Javier Culo shrieked (because that had been another thing that miffed him).

"I'm sorry, then," Dusty concluded with the small air he had left, "I don't recognize you at all. (Unless it's from the laundromat.)"

As his 30-year vendetta had centered around the red-haired man's recognizing him, and since the red-haired man clearly didn't, Javier Culo let Dusty go. The red-haired man coughed and sputtered for a while in the dooryard, then went back in to Roz, who kissed him, enfolded him, and said she would never drink Zima again. Javier Culo, meanwhile, decided he should get a job.

CHAPTER LXIII

DON'T YOU LOOK AT MY GIRLFRIEND

Do you think that the band lost a bet
In re: How laid could Supertramp get
When they wagered the farm
On Prog Rock's dark charm
And dependence on the clarinet?

CHAPTER LXIV

FLING IT AT THE DUMPSTER, MIJO

IT WASN'T UNTIL LATER, after Alice had gotten up and gone to work, that I opened my eyes again and heard the place settle around me. The housecleaner who lived upstairs and her adult sons were on the move, and soon their door opened and closed and I could hear the Mom thumping down the stairs by Alice's bedroom. She was heading off to her own job while the boys upstairs sugared up for a long day of XBox (I could feel the telltale bloops in my hair—they had their system hooked up to the stereo). Later the two biggest masses anyone ever called "mijo" would emerge onto the balcony to fling empty liter Coke bottles into the Dumpster by the alley, and I would watch their cigar ash drift down like we were Mt. St. Helens-adjacent rather than Culver City Forever.

I was alone in yet another girlfriend's apartment, feeling welcome enough to be naked under abundant bedspreads and duvets or whatever they're called, to creak barefoot along hardwood floors, soak the dishes, make coffee with the unfamiliar machine, press clean buttons on a nicer microwave. But do I throw the sheets in the wash? If they were my linens I'd want to sleep in them the next night, just to linger. But I'm a voluptuary. Results vary with Alice.

I definitely wasn't going to eat her food. We weren't at that place yet. Which also meant my soap wasn't in the shower. I washed with something lavender and nubbly and $3.50 a bar and shampoo'd with some pearlescent ooze belched from a squat, caked bottle with French cursive on the label. I emerged from my ablutions feeling clean, I guess, but her products were different from mine, and I was hesitant to go deep with any of her bathing tools. Then I dried myself on a towel that still smelled like her, like the decades-ago women's floors of freshman dorms. I savored the brief thrill of being a trespasser in her life.

I savored it because I think this feeling is running out of time. I've stockpiled a quarter century of apartments like this across the country. They don't change much, aside from a decrease in the age of the roommates. I used to exchange kitchen pleasantries with Irish girls in their 20s, then bearded recluses older than us, eating cereal in their rooms, and now they're teenagers who stay with their dads on the weekend. But yeah, I think it's going away. In two decades I went from Sinead's boyfriend to Sarah's partner to Mom's—. Well, Mom is in a weird place with that.

When there'd be a household outing, it used to be to the bar. Now it's to Family Fun World or Shakey's or mini-golf. In this period of my life I've gone on these journeys with a yogapant of single moms. The kid gets 9-dollar macaroni and cheese that costs a quarter at home and he still doesn't eat it. Or she tries to steal the fertile, swarming balls from the ball pit. Or I'm the bad guy for winning at air hockey. Her mom and I get watered-down drinks. I give him money for the arcade that he accepts tentatively, checking in with his mother that she's OK. Mom says I'm the best fuck she's ever had, and I clamp my hand over her mouth. No wonder the kid looks at me funny.

Alleys and little kitchen gardens and sometimes front yards. The bright silence of a California apartment complex weekday morning, strangely Puritan in that you know there's a lot of unemployed people around but they feel guilty playing their music while they should be working. Duplexes and neighbors on the other side of the wall. An uneasy feeling—not quite my place to do as I please despite having been told otherwise.

And while the roommate demographic changed, the level of squalor merely adjusted. I'm an adjunct professor in my 20s killing my girlfriend's cockroaches, I'm a divorced dad in my 40s putting together her daughter's bed. It seems tawdry, somehow, and incomplete. All over the world are boyfriends like me and the fellows upstairs: bass players, bloggers, guys who make animated GIFs. "This is my boyfriend. He does the font for memes part time? He's 50."

I hear the clock ticking, it's that quiet sometimes (Hector and Alex are going to Jack in the Box because the state now deposits unemployment funds on a Bank of America debit card and a text message told them that the money just hit). I could fight my way across the city to make a grilled cheese at home or I could just stay here, careful not to leave crumbs on the couch and maybe hang up her TV, tape down a floor runner. Things I should be doing with someone I'm married to. But this isn't New York—people my age build lives in apartments there; we settle for apartments here, and we suffer from a low-grade unhappiness about it, draining our batteries as the defeat constantly refreshes in the background.

My own job is thousands of miles away and I completed it, by FTP, last night. I'm done for the week. I inserted some code in a program that will be used in classroom software in Latvia. Talk about temporary. How long does *that* place have left?

I'm not going to be here when her son comes home. I'm a man older than his dad who now smells like his mom's soap. Maybe they do this all the time in France, or in group living situations in Berkeley, but down here it just seems gross, Bukowskian. I'd be able to see the awful poetry and sketchbook drawings coming out of the kid now, the ballpoint threatening to press through the paper, Mom saying, "Why don't you show Norman your art?" The kids and I looking at each other, both of us saying, "You're just like the last one."

I've received a key, and lock the place behind me. But I remove the key from my ring and slip it back through the mail slot. Through the window of a neighboring apartment I hear what sounds like a Santeria ritual. As I pass the next one down I hear some yapping dogs that suggests the place is rented by a family member of the manager. From the last apartment before the parking lot a woman emerges in front of me. She's in her mid-30's, tired, with a baby under one arm and a laundry basket under the other.

I hear myself say, "I can help you with one of those."

CHAPTER LXV

FLOAT AWAY TO HAPPYLAND

"Gower beats me and drinks Everclear,"
Said Half-Deaf George Bailey. "I fear
That I'll e'er be a drone
At the Building & Loan
But Violet's a sight for sore ear."

CHAPTER LXVI

NO STRANGER TO YOU AND ME

RAY FLOATED SLIGHTLY ABOVE the Earth. Nothing heroic, but just enough to free him from any static cling. In levitation lingo, this was known as Glancing, as it gave the levitator enough time to get back on the ground should a non-mystic pass by and do a double-take, or feel awkward. The Levitationists were the only religion that took into account other people's feelings.

He was pondering God. Again.

"If we look at the world and see everything as the result of an action," he thought, retracing steps in the air like he was trying to remember where he left his keys, "then every result has sprung from the Ur-Action of God."

Audrey walked into the spare room where Ray kept his keys and various fart-redolent mats (Ray farted as he levitated, and it made him feel like Yosemite Sam. He had detached from embarrassment, however). Ray briefly thought about landing, but how would his hasty thump reflect the new honesty in their relationship? Just because she couldn't get off the ground without a boost didn't mean he shouldn't feel free to hovercraft around the room, free of shame.

"This month's Westways came," she said, tossing the AAA magazine on the floor.

"Hey—" Ray said, teetering in the air, "could you just put it with all the other mail? I'm trying to keep this room free of everything except my keys and mats."

This was a new program, Ray knew, but he'd been able to keep the room swept and Spartan for nearly two weeks. A couple of weekends ago he'd embarked on a noble initiative to clear the room of a bunch of inkjet printers, Palm Pilots, cardboard boxes neither of them would ever use to ship Christmas presents or anything, a crockpot, a breadmaker, a juicer, and several generations of iPods, Androids, and even an HD-DVD player. *Ha ha!* Ray thought serenely. *What were we thinking?*

"Oh. Right," Audrey said. She left the room and Ray made it just past her fading footsteps before he crashed to the ground, distracted. He hoped she hadn't heard.

"Are you O.K.?" came Audrey's voice. She had been poised outside the door.

"Yeah," Ray said, but she hadn't waited for his reply.

That evening they chatted amiably through dinner. Afterwards he excused himself and levitated into the far upper corner of the spare room. Audrey called for him but he didn't answer. She entered the room below him, and he looked at her from her scalp to the top of her shoes.

For Audrey's part, she knew he was there. Only she understood her sense of peace when everyone around her was uncomfortable. She felt like the wandering eye of a hurricane, a barometric Sandy Duncan.

Ray floated down a few hours later. All this levitating was supposed to make him feel better, but what he really needed was some sleep.

In the bedroom the fan was lifting the sheet. It billowed above the foot of the bed. He reached down to touch the top of the sheet with his fingertips. He said, "This is the Result of something that started a long time ago."

"It looks like a ghost," said Audrey, behind him. "Maybe we're all dead."

CHAPTER LXVII

PRIORITIES

Granddad had money to spill
So he put Chick-fil-A in his will
His batter-fried views
Were assigned by Fox News
(Plus he was mentally ill.)

CHAPTER LXVIII

DISPOSAL

RAY WASN'T THE SAME person he was a decade ago. For one thing, he had probably sweated a self's worth of cheese in just the past year. "I don't know," he texted Frank (were they even friends, or did each just know so many things about the other man that there was no use making things up, which is something friends don't do, either?), "I'm thinking cremation, or Air Lock."

Frank was helping Ray with his New Hire paperwork, and they'd come to the Disposition of Remains part. Ray felt a number of emotions turning that page, including Fear of Commitment. And Guilt. Here was a company offering to do the noble work of getting rid of his corpse, and he was antsy about it? Maybe it had something to do with the fact that the laminator was overheating, so his interment would be settled before he got his orientation badge.

"I'm calling you," Frank texted, maneuvering around a big piece of chicken, apparently. "I just dropped a big piece of chicken on the screen and can't see."

Ray was also wary of letting Frank know how he wanted his soul's envelope to be dealt with. It seemed too intimate a fact for Frank to be in charge of. Frank, who was one of those people who used "your" incorrectly but who still made more money than Ray. Frank, who liked to say "Your gay" and you could hear the lack of an apostrophe just in the way he said it. Frank, who had taken Lotus Notes in high school to get out of taking French and who was therefore the only person at Blimp-Corp.edu who could enter paycheck information, and who became the Human Resources director because of it. Frank, who knew Ray's social security number and that he had a pre-existing condition (intermittent philtrum prolapse).

Ray was already staring at the device, but still jumped when it rang.

"Air Lock is an additional $10 per pay period," Frank was saying instead of Hello. "Cremation is free. Terrestrial Interment is free. Company cemetery near Dallas, with the full audiovisual fantasia teraflop coin thing, and/or whatever that evolves into, for 25 years."

"I can't possibly work here long enough to cover the cost of shooting my body into space and then releasing it from an Air Lock," Ray said. "Even if I work here 20 years, that's still ...just over five thousand bucks for a trip to space. I couldn't get up there alive for less than a million."

"Space travel gets less expensive every year," Frank said quickly. "Plus it's the perception of value that makes it expensive. It's five thousand because they make sure you're dead first and that you're not secretly enjoying it or learning anything from it. I mean, if your corporeal form retains any sense of dignity post-mortem, it's gonna have to recover big time from the way they get you up there."

Frank briefly described a procedure involving a German phrase that meant nose-to-asshole.

"It's not until the robots pop your nose out of the other guy that what's left of you can really revel in the majesty of the nearer recesses of Space," Frank said.

Ray was unconvinced, despite Frank's pitch. He chose cremation.

"It's your funeral," Frank said.

During Ray's time with the company, it turned out that one of the warehouse guys dropped dead, and he was one of the Air Lock disposals. That was when Frank's short-sighted scheme unraveled. He'd been collecting $260 a year each from about 80 employees, and when one of them kicked off, Frank would have the body cremated for free and then just leave the ashes in the oven, instead of transporting them to the South African Space Agency, as he'd told the families.

Frank told the authorities that with the first few he'd thrown the ashes really far from the top of a hill. Then he got lazy.

But that would be in a few years. Now Ray had shared with Frank the very personal news that, when he died, he wanted his body to be burned.

"Kind of a self-hating way to go," Frank said under his breath, but loud enough for Ray to hear, almost. "Too bad people can't make fun of you to death, or you'd probably choose that."

"What?"

"Nothing."

"Just curious," Ray asked, "what option did you choose?"

"Well, that's none of you're God Damn business, now, is it?" Frank said brightly.

Ten years ago Ray couldn't imagine the idea of being a company man, but now he was one. It wasn't bad. He'd get a vacation. He'd get this thing where they encourage you to eat salads. There'd be 45-year-olds, fresh from their morning jobs at a children's theatre, coming in to do chair massage every Thursday.

He couldn't put his finger on what was bothering him about doing a job he didn't want to do for people who might fire him at any moment, as opposed to not doing what he wanted to do anyway and being paid less. It was like he had to squint to see the difference.

He went to the bathroom and sat in a stall, checked messages on his phone, played a game with the sound off until the Wi-Fi cut out. Then he remembered to be in the present for a second and articulate what was bothering him.

"Oh yes," he concluded. "As long as I don't try, I can't experience failure. Of course it ends up being a long trudge through near-constant failure, but no one's going: Ha ha, *Failure*. So determining where my ashes are going to go pretty much locks me into a life of conspicuous Trying."

It was one of those disconcerting toilets that flushed as soon as thighs left the seat. At least he wouldn't have to worry about *that* when he was dead. He returned to the conference room where Frank waited.

"Oh. We'll need some of your urine," Frank said. "Well, a lot of your urine."

Ray made the common gesture indicating that he'd just been to the bathroom and wouldn't have any urine for a while.

"I'll leave some on the side of the building," he said.

CHAPTER LXIX

AT THE FT. McHENRY SMOKING AREA

"If we kept the chord structure the same,"
Said Francis Scott Key, "are you game
If I said that the gist
Was that the South simply missed
The flag with their horrible aim?"

CHAPTER LXX

LEGGY

RAY CONSIDERED THE IMPLICATIONS of someone so leggy. It was as if he'd finally heard, for the first time, a word he'd only read before, and the word sounded a lot different from how he'd mouthed it all this time. What did it really mean to be leggy? When he was a child, Ray thought that it meant having more than two legs. A spider was leggy. He wondered why the old men at the Damnucketville Social Club were getting so worked up over women who looked like spiders. Did they know yet another thing that Ray didn't?

As he grew, Ray became aware that some men liked certain parts of the female anatomy with greater intensity than they liked other parts. Of course, this was for entertainment purposes only. Some men were Leg Men, some were Hip Men, and some, Ray giggled nervously, were *Tube Men.* He had difficulty even typing it.

Ray wasn't the type to favor some parts over others; he was democratic. He took a gestaltist view of things, waiting for the parts to assemble into a whole. Or he might have been more of an anarchist, because there was a general lawlessness to what he liked or didn't like as much, depending on the day. This spared him the moral turmoil of having to stick a button on his jean jacket or loudly and publicly say things like, "I'm a Tube Man, myself" and only going to tube bars.

But Audrey changed everything. She was the type of woman who made you take sides. Sandinistas? Well are *you* going, Audrey? OK. What are the Sandinistas wearing these days? Audrey saw your confidence playing in the schoolyard and called it over to the chain link fence, dropped some PCP into its milk, and came back the next day with the good stuff. And soon your confidence was straddling the hoods of police cars, punching the windshields in. And, what's more, Audrey was leggy.

Leggy like you read about—in *medical journals*. Leggy like you expected to see snowcaps at the top of them, or an extra tablet of commandments stuck somewhere on the way down. Leggy like you'd need a "Star Trek" spinoff to explore the length of them. Finally, he understood. And here she was, talking to Ray.

"Is that your arm?" she asked.

"Sorry," said Ray, pulling his arm back into his own airplane seat. She was carrying a bomb, Ray predicted, but it wasn't in her shoes. She sat down and pushed the hard, cold airline grapes around her tray table.

"I think it's a shame that the passengers in Coach have to walk through First Class and see people sitting comfortably without thrombosis," she said. Ray felt ashamed, suddenly, that he'd paid the extra ungodly amount for the upgrade. Then he remembered that she was here, too, so there was no reason for shame. "You have to pay all this money just to have some dignity, and still the food is awful."

Ray's mind formed into an inner slack-jawed gape at the beauty of this woman, and yet he yearned for another time, and this wasn't the first time. Ray yearned for the time when if strangers talked to each other it was only friendly and didn't lead to worries of a pending invitation to a Bible Study or helmeting in the Men's room. And if he responded in kind, how would she take it? Was there a hint Ray was supposed to have picked up in those two sentences that, if he answered in just as innocuous a fashion, she would think him square, or a masher, or a Jedi? Ray himself wasn't the type of person to start conversations with strangers, simply because most of the conversations strangers had started with him were for motives other than curing boredom; it was a prejudice he had stuck by.

But here she was, chattering away, and Ray was chattering right back. The steward brought watered-down cocktails, and the in-flight movie droned soundlessly, as the two seatmates communicated only with each other. Her name was Audrey, and she was delighted that she didn't have to hit the ground running tomorrow, that she could watch cable in the hotel room or walk across the highway to Applebee's and tie one on if she wanted to, not being due at the conference center until Tuesday.

"Does Applebee's have a full bar?" she said. "Or any bar?"

Ray didn't know. What he said was, "It sounds like you've got your downtime accounted for, but there's one or two places around town that you might like—and I'm just guessing —better than Applebee's. Furthermore," he said, summoning courage, "I could take you there."

Audrey appraised bold Ray, winked, then got up suddenly.

"I've got to go to the bathroom," she said.

What the hell did that mean? Ray wondered. Who leaves an intriguing conversation like that to go to the bathroom? You hold it *in*, is what you do.

Ray wasn't a schmoozer. He didn't close deals this way. Suggesting an Applebee's alternative was off-brand for him, but also a Big Step. He slumped in his chair, both winded with the effort and confused that Audrey was gone. He took a deep breath, sighing heavily.

And that's when he noticed that the seat Audrey had vacated was redolent of her farts, and he saw that a grape had rolled into her buttockdivot. To her credit, Ray thought, Audrey had probably held on as long as she could before excusing herself. And he saw the dilemma she must have been in: stay and chat and risk her bowels evacuating or leave quickly and hope her new friend was just a mouth breather?

Ray's better angels blessed Audrey for the tough choices before her, but he was still miffed that she'd been flatulent on a plane, and that she'd dropped a perfectly good grape in its essence. It was a short flight, and there were even fewer grapes. There was a drought on.

Had Ray not done what he did, he would have seen Audrey returning from the bathroom, a spring in her step, a breeziness that other men down the aisle certainly noticed.

But Ray was pretending to be asleep.

"*I'm not wearing any panties*," Audrey said, sitting down and inadvertently hoovering up a grape, but Ray was affecting some light snores.

Later, as the plane pulled into the gate, he pretended to be dead.

CHAPTER LXXI

MIRACLE TOURISM

My local patisserie's cred
Shot up when the Virgin Mom's head
Appeared not on just
The day-old pie crust
But all the good multigrain bread.

CHAPTER LXXII

THE DUMB WAY

OUR SUBSTITUTE SECOND GRADE TEACHER strode purposefully to the chalkboard. He smirked at the cursive letters arranged above it, capital and minuscule, trailing off to the cloakroom. The Qs, which always irritated him, were arranged on a piece of construction paper that was drooping in the northwest corner. He resecured the tape, getting some chalkdust on his pits, but the Qs drooped even more later. (There would be no later.)

"It's 9:35," he said, when we were all in our seats, "you should have been back from the cloakroom five - "

"Cloakroom?" John said.

"What's a cloakroom?" said Kelly Ann.

"*Cloakroom*?" I said.

"Hey." the substitute teacher said. "You know what a cloakroom is."

"You mean the *coat* room?" Scott said.

"You knew what I was talking about!" he cried. That shocked us a little, because they usually didn't raise their voices so quickly. But he was a sub, and he walked in there really cocky, smirking at our letters. Who did he think he was? "Does somebody want to go sit in the corner?"

We were such bastards. We all got up and pushed and shoved each other on our way to the corner, where there was a little stool, a plant, and a poster of a kitten who had gotten into the milk. We elbowed each other out of the way, but finally Jackie and Heather were on the stool together. The substitute teacher gently moved them off, stirring Jackie to fall on the floor and start wailing as a formality, and then shooed us back to our seats.

We gave the guy no peace all the way up to recess. In math, we giggled when he said "divisor" even though we'd heard it from Miss Cullen a hundred times. In science I kept sticking straws up my nose. And in music (the music teacher didn't show up and our sub lost his only chance for a break) we giggled when he sang "Yellow Submarine" to us. He probably liked the song before, but we made him feel like shit. When recess rolled around, he advised us to move quickly, quietly, and in single-file when we were using the stairwell.

"Stairwell?"

"Single file?"

"*Stairwell*?"

"Listen!" he yelled (and they all yelled, even the good ones, and they think we won't remember because we were seven, but we do), "You know exactly what I'm talking about! Don't repeat it like you're monkeys!" This caused us all to start jumping around like monkeys (or something, because some of us were just jumping around like kids). And then he said: "Remember. I'm the teacher and you're the pupil."

(Such joy inhabited us.)

"Pupil?" Andrea said (and we can see why).

"*Pupil*?" said Demetrius.

Some of us started acting it out, running around the room like we were pupils, drooling and hanging our tongues out. That was one we legitimately didn't know. He could've said, "I'm your pedophile" and we would've done the same thing.

Out in the recess yard, Jeff waited for me, to punch me. He said, "Are we gonna fight today?"

My mother, who had counseled me on such matters, had said that I should answer that question with: "The smart way or the dumb way?" The smart way was to submit to a test of mental skill, like Chinese Checkers, my mother said, "Mental like" and the dumb way was, obviously, to get my ass kicked. How could anyone possibly choose the dumb way? Then I would win in any smart way I chose. My mother was a genius! Armed thusly, I said to Jeff:

"The smart way or the dumb way?"

Jeff sighed like the substitute teacher did when he knew and we knew that we were just being assholes. "The dumb way," he said after not much time at all, but then the bell rang.

CHAPTER LXXIII

SYMPATHY FOR THE DAUPHIN

"With days elapsed since your last meal,
I'll make with you rabble a deal:
Do not interrupt
The Dauphin til he's supped—
Believe me, he knows how you feel."

CHAPTER LXXIV

LEMON CONSENT

DOWN THE ALLEY, BETWEEN the streets, in a sort of gully that makes an island of these two houses, is a lemon tree in a slim side yard. Each night I walk past it, my lungs already full of Night Blooming Jasmine, Hopeful, and I can almost see the lemons growing bigger, threatening to drop and be destroyed, with no one bothering to pick them before that happens. I resolve one night that I will stop by the house the next morning, 10-cent grocery bag folded in my pocket, and politely ask at the door if I can simply reach up and pick a dozen or so lemons.

I know everything that can go wrong. I can arrive to receive no answer to my knock but, since I'm already in the yard and since I've never seen any evidence of those lemons being picked—just rotted off the branches into the gully—in three years, I wander over to the tree. But then someone raps at the window and tells me to get out. Or the door is opened by a tiny person who aggressively doesn't understand a thing I say to him but breathes, patiently, perhaps waiting for his God to come and take me off his doorstep. Words like "lemon" and "tree" and "*limon*" and "*baum*" and "*arbor*" and "*douche*." He just stares at me. Finally I resolve that this is some game we're playing and I take my bag to the tree but he is following with some garden implement shouting "No! No!" and I leave. Or, worse, I plead my case to a frowning woman who listens to my request and simply says, "No, we don't *give away* our lemons," as if I'm a vagrant who just asked for her plasma.

There are other, more complex scenarios in which I'm refused but reply, "If I pick those lemons then they won't rot in the alley" or "Not once in the three years that I've been walking by here has a single person picked a lemon from that tree" or "*Why even have a lemon tree then*?"

But arguing after someone says No seems rude. And yet the balance will have shifted so that I'm suddenly a neighborhood menace, eyeing the forbidden tree as I walk past, the homeowners behind their blinds but me just Out There in the World, ready to take what isn't mine, resentful and ominous. They'll whisper to the neighbors that I asked for their lemons, won't let their children play with mine, what with the scurvy.

Thus prepared for any eventuality except the one I am about to encounter, the next morning I knock on the door. The woman who answers isn't wearing any pants.

"Good morning!" I say. "I'm your neighbor from down the street on Gerald Ford. Is it allright if I pick about a dozen of your lemons?"

"I don't know," she says thickly, her whole face seeming to slide down to the left but catch on some peg like a heavy bathrobe. "Nobody has touched those lemons."

"I noticed that," I say. "I make lemonade, and lemon sugar scrub from the peels, and candied lemon, and I even freshen up the kitchen and bathroom with whatever's left. I use the whole thing."

She has pooped herself.

"I'm like a *Lemonavajo*," I continue. The term still delights me and, it seems, no one else. The woman and I look at each other frankly.

"I even make my own limoncello," I say. "I get some 151 and some sugar and I zest the lemons and you put it in a glass jar for about a month, and—all my friends like it."

Maybe it's my upbringing. I was told not to stare. Somewhere in English class this got prettified to Don't State the Obvious. And I've been there—I remember walking into kindergarten having stepped in something and all my classmates falling over themselves to point it out. So the lady shat herself. So what? It's her house and the lemons aren't inside with her but out where I am.

But something else from English class. Some "White Man's Burden" thing (but she's whiter than I am)? Perhaps something from "Heart of Darkness" (Nope. No boats)? Oh:

She is growling like a mad dog, a mad dog loping down the street, thick and ropy, looking at me under her heavy brows. Calpurnia is about to call Heck Tate to come shoot it. But I'm still Dill to the lemons that are the Finches. Go set a watchman on that analogy.

I can see why no one picks the lemons; if this is what she's like in the doorway, how must she be in the yard? I start to formulate an exit strategy.

But she is at me now, all teeth and eye sockets and melon body spray and a too-small Cheap Trick t-shirt and I know what to do. I not-unkindly grab a handful of her hair and walk her back inside, keeping her at arm's length. The living room is cool and pleasant. Two comfortable couches on a shining brown hardwood floor. A reasonably-sized flat screen TV over the mantelpiece, positioned for occasional viewing rather than every night's 6-2 a.m. shift. A single indifferent cat, a bird in a cage, and a stack of bodies in the corner. Many genders and races. A neat little pile of recycled bags, here and there a backpack, and one of those plastic handbaskets someone had managed to get out of Ralph's all in a pyramid in the opposite corner.

"Oh, I get it," I say. "Lemons are a thing now."

"Yeah," she says, coming toward me. She's wearing black socks. "People see a lemon tree, they're all like, 'Oh, I'll ask that person for all her lemons' when they can go to Trader Joe's and get a bunch of them - "

"Whoa," I say. "But they're so expensive - "

"Well even if they weren't expensive, you wouldn't buy them. But you see them in someone's yard - "

"I just thought I'd ask you," I say. "I didn't want to be like the guys rooting through the garbage at 2 a.m., sneaky. At least, you know, give you the benefit - "

"Shut up," she says, falling heavily on a pair of middling-meaty knees. "I'm so tired."

"OK," I say, backing up. "I'm just going to go take those lemons because I can use them. I'll bring you some limoncello in a month. I really appreciate it. You should clean off your legs, though."

"OK."

I back out, closing the door behind me. I think it would be uncool for her to see me calling the police, so I make my way around to the side yard and deftly snap about 14 good-sized lemons from the low branches. I peek into the window and she has scrambled to the top of the mound of bodies and is howling away.

I don't know her name, so I decide I'll call her Karen. I've known several Karens in my life. One is the secretary to an abortionist, the other is a cancer ward clown. Good people. Both fond of pets, as I recall from their Facebook updates.

"Thanks, Karen!" I say.

That night I clear off the kitchen table, gather the cutting board, a cheapo manual juicer, various bowls and bottles, a bag of sugar and everything that I can think of to help me make the most of these lemons.

Then I think of Karen, who probably would have murdered me had it not been for my being polite. Befecaled, half naked, feral Karen.

I'm learning to be more picky, I think.

CHAPTER LXXV

HER NAME WAS BATHSHEBA

Each morning King David would check
For the chick tanning up on her deck
She was so pretty that
He almost begat
All over her face, hair, and neck.

CHAPTER LXXVI

DING DONG

SWALLOWING HARD, squinting several times, and clearing his throat, spoke Ray thus to Audrey:

"Will you marry me?"

It had taken him awhile to get here. Their relationship had changed, had—oh my god: Crucible? Chrysalis? When mosquitoes lay eggs in the cat dish and there's maggots?—gone from one thing to another and they had weathered this together so it was meant to be. Ray was grayer. Audrey was grayer (but in the face). The cat had been taken away by maggots like it was Magical Cat Realism in sweaty cat banana republics where people cooked with their tears and whatnot and didn't mind a little padding around the thighs and eventually got around to reading "A Hundred Years of I'm Never Getting Another Cat."

So with the lack of anyone else staying around for a paragraph like that, Ray popped the question to Audrey, who said (they all said):

"It's your funeral."

"Is that a yes?"

Ray's proposal hadn't been accepted in the way he would have liked. He had always been the romantic one, and Audrey had always been, well, Audrey had always been the one to act as if it were a personal favor if she didn't slit her own throat and die right in front of you.

He went on gamely. "Should we elope or have a big wedding?"

"Please yourself."

"I'd like at least a few people there," Ray said, pulling out his notebook, "and there's a French Horn solo that I think would be lovely, and maybe if we did it in the fall — "

"Ray?" (it was Audrey).

"Yes, sweetheart?"

"If I had a scrotum—and who says I don't—I would rather be bootkicked in it by lumberjacks than call any attention to our misguided love for each other."

"OK, sure." (It was a relief to get anything definite out of her.)

Later that night, drinking like a bootkicking-weary lumberjack, Ray related the good news to his buddies at the Trainwreck Lounge.

"And she's a safe driver," he was saying, after an uncomfortable silence.

"Well, Ray my lad," said Frank, clapping him on the back, "now that you're entering the world of responsible men, I feel it's my duty as the senior account rep at Spayborn and Helme to illuminate to the best of my ability the world of women."

Ray didn't want Frank to do this 1.) because he wanted it all to remain a sweet mystery until his wedding night and 2.) because Frank was known to fuck sheep. But Frank was working up to an epic recitation:

"Women like to be grazed lightly, with knuckles, under the chin," he said. "They love Twinkies and Ding Dongs. They enjoy the films of Drew Barrymore. They think animals are capable of love. They would rather vacuum a rug than take a punch in the gut for America. They are fonder of sprouts than we are. They aren't as into lesbo scenes as certain magazines would suggest. In general they type and parallel park better. They are made entirely of clams."

At this last bit of information Ray stopped jotting down Frank's words.

"It's true," Frank said, smiling at Ray's disbelief, "ask any woman."

Bette, Ray's boss, happened to be in the bar with a client. "Sorry to bother you, Bette," Ray said, "but Frank says all women are made of clams."

"Not the same species and strain of clams, of course," Bette said, looking embarrassed but good-natured, "but clams nonetheless."

I don't get it, Ray thought.

That night he dropped by Audrey's mother's house. Audrey was staying there while the government removed several million suspicious ball bearings from the hassock in her apartment. "I need to know," he said, breathless from the run and his own confusion, "do you love me?"

"No," Audrey said, "I love Twinkies and Ding Dongs, but thank you for asking."

CHAPTER LXXVII

SOURCE TEXT: ADULTERY ATTRACTS SHARKS

Straight into her pants like a rook
Jumps Hooper at Ellen's sly look
Their vile assignation
Mocks your chaste beach vacation
Thus why he must die in the book.

CHAPTER LXXVIII

DIPLOMACY

IT WAS PRETTY LATE already, and I didn't want to be there. I was doing my best to keep the goodbyes short. Meanwhile, I had to make sure that none of the rancor I felt would bubble up. Let's just say the bucket of amicable goodwill was about empty. But that's *Home* me. *Work* me has serious strategic reserves. This sort of balancing act defines my job; I am a pro at making people feel better about themselves.

"Wish you could stay longer," my host—a nobleman from some dusty place where they cut your hands off when that sort of thing needs to happen in order to save the rest of your arm and it's all paid for by the government and you don't drop dead from overwork because you actually have vacations even if you're just the guy who brushes butter onto the beignets or lagniappes or whatever the fuck— said.

"I would if your state functions didn't *suck ass*," I replied, mollifying him.

I am weary of my job butting into my personal life. Just as a doctor will shrivel a little at being asked for medical advice at parties, or a celebrity can't visit her family without being hounded for autographs, I wish I could just once go somewhere not job-related and be free of having to behave diplomatically. Or—you know what?—go to a function that *is* job-related and not be some stupid perpetual pleasantries monkey.

Just the other day I went to the pool store for a bucket of chlorine. I was in my shorts and sunglasses, baseball cap pulled backwards, etc., the full weekend-casual loafing outfit. Yet here was this guy at the counter demanding I lay some smooth politesse on him.

"Will that be all?" he goes.

"Fuck you, cow." I said, biting my tongue to keep from being rude. Can't people tell that I'm not working?

At the U.N. I'm all business. Some blowhard from the Third World wants to vent, I'm right there. I even printed up a little sign that says Third World Venting Room on my closet and I just send them in there when my in-ear Bluetooth translator gets waxy. Banana republics squabbling over a piece of dirt that's only visible at low tide? They send me. I don't mind having mud slung at me—that's my job. Just give me my weekend for Pete's sake.

Wednesday afternoon we hosted some tribal chieftains from West Africa. Pretty touchy stuff. Warlords from way back who'd only agreed to come to arbitration after some heavy finessing. I began the summit by acknowledging the great show of good faith on all parties' parts just to be there. Eschewing introductions to give the participants an idea that the U.N. was well-versed in their very personal disputes, we began the meeting in earnest.

"Listen *Pendejos*: My god can kick the shit out of your god, and I don't even believe in God," was how I started, and immediately got their full attention. "And another thing," I said, absently playing with my laser pointer by focusing it briefly on each of the chieftains' foreheads, "this is the goddamn U.N. in the goddamn United States of America: our unpaid membership dues alone is greater than the revenue from each of your three biggest exports for the past fifty years. Now don't you see how trivial your little backwater tiff is? Mosquito eggs in the cat dish, gentlemen."

(One of the warlords was technically a queen, but I didn't care.)

Mine is a delicate job, and I put a lot of work each and every weekday into easing tensions and resolving conflicts. Why can't people let me cut loose when I punch out on Friday?

Even my wife, who should know better, won't even give me a moment's peace. "Carl," she said when I got home on the last train at the end of a grueling week, "the paperboy is charging us for the two weeks we were at my mother's. Can you talk to him, because I just get too angry."

Too angry? *She* was angry? What did *she* do all week that would stress her out to the point she couldn't talk to the frigging paperboy? I felt a familiar vein groundhogging on my forehead, but I pushed it back with my thumb. The good thing about me is that I only stay angry at such indiscretions for a moment. I was immediately back in diplomat's trim, and I drove over to Jared's house to have a little talk with him, and his parents if they were around.

Turns out the whole family was there. They were having a barbecue out back, so I didn't want to make a big deal out of anything; I just wanted to resolve the situation and go back home for a leisurely swim, a beer, and then bed.

"Your cocksmoking son's trying to jew my wife out of two bits for that retarded paper," I said. "That paper's so retarded, I want to throw up. And your son's a little cocksmoker. In fact, your son is a world-class queef-smoking quahog." That's right: I said "quahog." Because we were in Providence. Had Jared lived in Woonsocket I would have said something about CVS. Like their shitty candy section.

Following assurances all around that it would never happen again, I drove home. Mary had a fantastic light tossed salad for me, which I ate before a relaxing swim. It's a time like this that I really enjoy my life, am thankful for the tough Jesuit education I got, and know that things aren't nearly as bad as I make them out to be.

CHAPTER LXXIX

THE LONELY WHALE

Before the last ice age receded
A whale swam to Utah unheeded
So softly he weeps
In the sub-Zion deep
That I worry he's feeling defeated.

CHAPTER LXXX

CREDIT

RAY'S HEART SLAPPED A shuffling rhythm, syncopating a martial beat every now and then with the help of his mitral valve prolapse. Audrey sat across the table, rearranging the pegs in the homespun mass-produced puzzle she'd swiped from the Bogue Chitto Cracker Barrel. The waitress came by. So this was Frank's new love interest. She had a forehead so high you could show the restored "Lawrence of Arabia" on it, but where Charles Manson would have put a swastika, she was wearing a frown.

"Your credit card has been rejected," she said, making no attempt to be discreet in the quiet restaurant. "Do you want to pay cash, or?" Actually, Ray wanted to use another credit card. He'd given her the wrong one, the one for the pricy feed store up in the hills. Of course it had been rejected. What bugged Ray was that she thought he *hadn't* made a mistake, that in fact he'd wanted to pay for their Valentine's Day meal with his Barn Club card.

"Sorry," Ray said, as Audrey looked up from her tiramisu. (*Tiramisu a new asshole*—Ray thought), "why don't you take this one?"

"We can't take another credit card if one has been rejected," the waitress said, a little louder. Ray would have to make a point to congratulate Frank on picking another winner.

"So what was the 'or' for?" Ray asked.

"Pardon?" Frank's Awful Squeeze replied. Ray didn't like the way she pronounced the word. She pronounced the schwa like a u, and gave both syllables equal emphasis. If she could be so fair to the syllables, why couldn't she cut Ray some goddamn slack?

"You asked me if I wanted to pay cash *or-*?" Ray replied. "Since I can't pay with another credit card, what is the other option you were about to introduce with the Or?"

—"Ray," Audrey said quietly.

"I think you're mistaken," the waitress said.

"But I'm not." Ray said.—

"Listen. There's an ATM right over there," Audrey said, "Why don't you just go there?"

"It'll charge me two bucks. Why can't you just take another credit card?" Ray wondered why things had to be so hard. It always had to be a struggle.

At that moment Frank walked in. He kissed the Battlestar Galactica-faced waitress and sat down with them.

"So what's the problem?"

Ray felt the second card being taken out of his hand. The waitress walked a few feet away to the machine and returned quickly, so Ray had nothing to say to Frank.

"You're all set," she said.

It was raining outside, and it would be a cold dash back to work, where Bette was eating her lunch of bagged soup alone. Ray signed the slip and wrote in a standard tip for the waitress, because he knew he'd have to come back.

CHAPTER LXXXI

THE DECADE IN WHICH WE LEARNED PURSER

Ten years gone awry of the plan
Were the 70s, joining Iran
Were fashion-plate pimps
And co-pilot chimps
But how to explain Steely Dan?

CHAPTER LXXXII

MEET THE SUSSKINDS

ALAN AND TRONDRA are siblings wandering through a bleak post-apocalyptic landscape. Trondra is somehow incapacitated so Alan must drag, carry, or roll her wherever they go. As light dawns on the stage, we find them at a crossroads.

TRONDRA
Where do we go? Where do we go now, Alan? Where do we go?

ALAN
I can't see through this soup. If the mountains are still on our right...I just can't see.

TRONDRA
We're not evolving fast enough, then. The world did its part. Now we have to respond.

TRONDRA strains, as if trying to pop out an extra eye from her forehead.

TRONDRA (cont'd)
You see anything? Anything pop out? I was thinking the world wanted me to pop out a new eye.

ALAN
It's a blackhead. Or a vein. It *might* be an eye.

TRONDRA
Well let's see what it turns into...

TRONDRA looks forlorn, suddenly, and begins to cry. ALAN tries to comfort her.

ALAN
It always clears up right after Explosion Time.

TRONDRA
I'm just sick of pooping blocks every time I try to evolve.

From under her skirt, TRONDRA pulls a makeshift catheter, which in her case is a Ziploc bag with some straws attached. Inside the bag is a bunch of multi-colored blocks, which she pours on the ground. THEY fight as ALAN tries to pick them up.

ALAN
Stop! Stop smearing them! This is how it started!

TRONDRA
It doesn't matter! They're just blocks!

ALAN
You don't know if you're pooping! You don't know what they are!

TRONDRA
They're *blocks*! And I *shit* them! I *shit* them, Alan! I know what part of me they come from!

ALAN

Why do you talk like that? Oh, God, Trondra! Each one is...so special.

ALAN has successfully restricted TRONDRA with his body and has gathered the blocks up despite her efforts, but now they are so close to one another that their panting and heaving have taken on extra significance.

TRONDRA

It's all right, Alan.

ALAN

It's wrong, what we do.

TRONDRA

We're making the rules now. We don't need these names. We don't need to be the Susskinds anymore. We're not carrying on the family name...

ALAN

We're still speaking English, right? I still wear slacks, right? You're wearing a skirt—

TRONDRA

That's right. I'm wearing a skirt...

ALAN

This is still America—

TRONDRA

And you're the president, Alan. You're the president. Now shoot some poop blocks into your disabled sister.

ALAN breaks free of their embrace.

ALAN
O tempora! O mores!

TRONDRA
Don't run away! It's almost Explosion Time!

ALAN has deposited the blocks into his knapsack, and now reveals that it is full of blocks.

ALAN
I've saved these.

TRONDRA
Oh, Alan, they're beautiful.

ALAN
I've...named them.

ALAN begins building a castle from the blocks. As he places each one, he lovingly and deliberately utters its name. TRONDRA begins to speak once he's made it through about 20 names.

ALAN (cont'd)
I call this one Lemmy. This one's Porthos. Grandizer. Danguard Ace. Li'l Em'ly. Dill. Geddy. Brown Jenkin. Chief Brody. Herve. Grover. Cicciolina. Baby Gangster. Left Eye. Guinevere. Backyardigan. Bombaclot. Pliny the Elder (he was the first one). Tiny Pliny. Gladstone.

Cromwell. Armo. Xiuxia. Radagast. Justin Hayward. Che. Amerigo. Esteban. Trondrita. Blocky...

TRONDRA

When I woke up last Thursday, I didn't put on my heels. I thought, "If they give me trouble about wearing sneakers, I'll take the writeup." But it's as if everyone was thinking the same way. Everyone was wearing sneakers. We had drinks during lunch. I left a $20 tip on a $30 bill. When it got dark at 3 o'clock, no one was surprised. We got up from our desks and proceeded in an orderly fashion to the street. We all looked up at the same time. It was a bright blue sky, and then it got dark. I was scared when the first few got sucked up, but then I just watched them whoosh into the sky. Just before they disappeared, they'd light up. First it was Human Resources, then Accounting, then IT, then the housekeeping ladies. Their clothes would stand up for a second, all the buttons buttoned, all the laces tied, and then just crumple because there was no body there. It started to sound like bells, but it was just the jewelry falling and clinking into the gutter. When it was over, I thought I was the only one left. Then you came. Then you came, Alan. I saw you in the distance when the cafeteria staff lit up. You were still there.

ALAN puts the finishing touches on his building.

ALAN

....Magilla, Clytemnestra, and Sweet Barbaro. Barbaro, you could have won it all.

TRONDRA

It's magnificent.

ALAN

You see, there has to be a reason we're still here. And I don't think evolution was ever elegant. But do you know why these are so pointy?

I think it's because we're not supposed to eat them, Trondra. And you have to admit the colors are both beautiful and basic. They're satisfying.

TRONDRA
I thought you'd be ashamed.

ALAN
That's going away, like when yesterday I sneezed and we determined it was my appendix that came out. I'm gonna feel weird whenever that feeling comes over us and then blocks come out of you. I can't lie. But by the next Explosion Time, I think you'll have an extra eye and whatever is going on on my back is going to be wings.

TRONDRA
Wings?

ALAN
Or wheels, or some lights, or maybe something that gives me suction, I don't know. But something is going on back there. You just keep making blocks, and stop saying you're pooping them, because I think that's not what's really happening.

TRONDRA
No, it isn't. They come from another place.

ALAN
I knew it.

TRONDRA
I'm not ready to show you yet.

ALAN
You don't need to prove anything to me.

TRONDRA
It's like a pussy, but it has flowers in it.

ALAN
No doubt.

The lights dim, there is a rumble in the distance. It's Explosion Time.

TRONDRA
It's Explosion Time, Alan.

ALAN
I wouldn't want to spend it with anyone else.

TRONDRA
I can't wait to see what you'll be.

ALAN
Maybe a duck.

BLACKOUT

CHAPTER LXXXIII

WHAT'S YOUR SECRET?

Each year I salute with a quaff
From an 1810 Puptibiboiffe
As my dark arts erase
All the age from my face
And I wait for the gauze to come off.

CHAPTER LXXXIV

IMPERATOR

WE WERE AWARE OF THE COMET for about three years before it hit us. It started popping up in scientific journals, then quickly spread to men's magazines with a science section, the internet, late night monologues, and then, finally, Audrey said she'd Heard someone talking about a comet or something and Why hadn't she Heard about this before and It's probably because I have better things to do like Live My Life, etc. By then not only was it too late (it was always too late) but everyone knew it was too late. The comet would hit sometime in the first week of September, three years from now, and that would be It.

Of the many cool things that resulted from "Comet Period," one of the first was its name. Some scholar named it Imperator, from the badass salute of soon-to-be-yoked-or-decimated Roman conquerees: "Ave, Imperator, morituri te salutant," or "Hey, Big Man, we who are about to die salute you." In kindergarten classes all over the world, kids called the comet "Morey Torey" and drew it with gritted teeth and a determined look on its face, as if destroying the world would ease Morey's constipation.

People took it different ways but, believe it or not, civilization continued unabated with only literary allusions to anarchy. Donald Trump tweeted: "The Bible predicted chaos and this is what we get? Pathetic."

But why go crazy? There was no profit in it. The elevator wasn't trying to break anyone down—a comet was going to destroy the elevator, the low-rise apartment building it was in, and every Otis alive or dead. The world was going to become perfect in three years, with no one going crazy to make a point, and then it would be destroyed.

Ray thought: if Jesus really wanted to please His Dad, He would have told everyone that the world was going to end in two weeks and then followed through on it. People would have towed the line, I assure you.

People began taking vacations and visiting their families. People spent less time at work, but still showed up. The President said, "I have a mistress whose stretch marks are perfect to snort coke out of" in the State of the Union address, and everyone laughed, both sides of the aisle, some Senators high-fiving. Someone even put it on a t-shirt. People got fatter, or skinnier, or had sex more, or dropped out of college, or cloned babies, and just didn't waste their time worrying about it. What have you always wanted to do? "Clone a baby." All right then: for Christ's sake Do It.

Religious types clucked knowingly and that was fine. Teachers taught Tony Hillerman, Joseph Wambaugh, and Erma Bombeck in school. Why not? They were awesome.

But Audrey and Ray were going through a tough time. The comet's impending arrival only strengthened her argument that she should see other people before she died. Ray kept telling her their relationship couldn't take it. "When a fisherman isn't at sea, he's mending his nets," she said cryptically. Ray responded, "Why should the shepherd fuck the sheepdog when he's got all those sheep?" Two could be cryptic, Ray thought, putting it on a t-shirt.

A few weeks from impact, gravity became all weird. Golf drives became longer, flapjacks in maple syrup commercials soared hundreds of feet above the loggers' picnic tables, and some breaching whales just floated off. Audrey was doing calisthenics in the park when Ray told her it was OK with him if she started playing the field. She stopped her jumping jacks, picked up her copy of "The Grass Is Always Greener over the Septic Tank," said, "This will be wonderful for us," and trotted off. Ray didn't see her again for a long time.

As Imperator approached, it was all quiet contemplation for me, letting the dishes pile up a little in the sink, allowing the dog to eat food out of my mouth because he clearly wanted to, and listening to those old songs I made on my four-track, like "Ozzy's Brain," "Still Lookin' for It (Your Love, Woman)," and my cover of "Flesh for Fantasy." There was a pretty big gathering on the beach as Labor Day approached, and I went down there a couple of times. People were starting to get a little antsy, and one time I saw some kid trying to make out with this girl who didn't want him to and a bunch of us went over there and told him to knock it off and he did. But other than that it was boring.

The day before Zero, Audrey and I hooked up. I was into Audrey from way back and was always trying to hang around her but there was Ray, and she acted as if I were a bug. But there was a little energy there, too. So now, at the end of all things, she was finally letting her guard down.

When you think about it, people with death sentences rarely have both freedom and health. Maybe they're healthy but on death row, or maybe they have their freedom but their illness prevents them from enjoying it. During the Comet Period, suddenly those refrigerator magnets that read "Live as if it's your last day on Earth" became *hilarious*. With three years to play around with, priorities could be considered soberly.

It kind of made you feel sorry for people who, in the past, had died without knowing it was going to happen eventually.

Imperator arrived (The night before: Crash Test Dummies/Decemberists deathmatch! Peter Gabriel returns to Genesis! Bill Ward on drums! Phil Collins plays for Sabbath! Rihanna and Chris Brown reunion where she beats the shit out of him! Coldplay and Radiohead reveal they are the same band! Bruno Mars and Lenny Kravitz and Carlos Santana and Pitbull and—huh?—Avril Lavigne on ESPN2!) and, inexplicably, only killed vegetarians who smoked. A lot of self-righteous closet smokers were outed in that holy fire, and generally people were happy to be rid of them, even at a federal level.

But on September 7, half a billion people committed suicide, just feeling exhausted and robbed. This was the segment of the population for whom the re-imposition of an open-ended era of being reasonable was just too much.

Ray, Audrey, and I still had to work together, but we didn't talk about Audrey's and my hookup. I must know half a dozen couples that had to try to close the barn door again, as it were. That would be an interesting documentary, you know? All the unexpected fallout from people who thought they were about to die, but didn't.

I think that sort of thing must have happened all over the world; people with the funny hair, the blue gods, bones in their noses, etc., waking up from it all, too scared to commit suicide, so, like me, they washed the dishes and took up with Shirley.

CHAPTER LXXXV

CROSSFIT EVANGELIST

In a stroke of great IOC branding
That defied secular understanding
Jesus came back
Bronzed in shotput and track
And on balance beam? Stuck every landing.

CHAPTER LXXXVI

ALAIN AND THE NUNS

WE AGREE THAT it took some time to get the boat launched and the pufferfish removed from Alain. We are in agreement also about the amount of time the souffle took to rise, and the darkness that followed. All over Canada the children wept of the tears, and *maman* could not keep them beavers from nibbling, nibbling the church down.

Francois-of-the-Canoe emerged from the river with them pelts and they did warm him, though they were wet there. With his pipe he called the young ones and they followed him, down to the circle under the trees, and they listened there to Francois as he recounted the journey across the pelty sea in their pelty boats there, with nothing to sustain them but thoughts of Paris when the cheese was ready, and some fat olives from the trees there where the hills were all grassy with the four-legged pre-pelts there. It was when Alain crept up that the pufferfish launched itself from the river there and tried to strangle Alain, because the whole world likes a good story.

What had enmaddened the pufferfish? The grandmothers say different things. The pufferfish was naturally nasty, some say. Others say that Alain challenged the pufferfish with his smell. Alain wafted many things depending on the day, and sometimes the bears would come down from Mt. Jen-Jen and rut in the streets when Alain was but breakfasting there.

Still others say that *Dieu* Himself commanded the pufferfish to counter Alain's prode, because the latter was getting too big for his britches, they said. *Cluk Cluk*, the grandmothers would always conclude, his *maman* was a gentle pigeon.

Francois-of-the-Canoe leaned forward, and the children there leaned forward, and their heads went Conk together there, and they rolled back into the knees of the fat uncles standing around the circle, because not one of the uncles trusted Francois-of-the-Canoe and his stories, or Fuck the stories, the uncles thought, Who can trust Francois-of-the-Canoe? But even the uncles wanted to hear more about the mighty and doomed Alain, for surely that was where the story was headed.

Alain and the pufferfish wrestled for two days and three nights, double occupancy in the fermenting hills of the north camps there. Between the rivers they strove, and through them, and up the other banks. On Sunday they went to mass at Notre Dame de Portage but got right back into it after the recessional. The burly bearded *voyageurs* saw a shadow coming over the hill on the third day and strained to see through their toxoplasmosis. It was Alain, God Save Us! But the pufferfish had taken a terrible toll.

He was weary unto death, whispered Francois-of-the-Canoe, and the children trembled. The uncles hunkered down, rapt, finally not caring that Francois-of-the-Canoe's fly had been gaping open the whole time. The stern Alain, Alain d'Avoirdupois, son of the jolly old Messr. Barnois, who gave the milk to the seagulls that day, *Oh Alain! What happened to poor Alain?* the children cried.

Well, Francois-of-the-Canoe said, straightening up, when he was young, Alain was very good to the nuns. It is always important to be good to the nuns, children, Francois-of-the-Canoe said firmly, because now the beleaguered Alain was in dire need of them there. Over the opposite hill, coming all the way from Montreal God Bless It, Francois-of-the-Canoe cried, his voice rising, came a floe of nuns in full chain mail, their maces whistling eerie theremin dirges across the valley. At the very sound of them, and indeed at the slightest whiff of their severe deodorant-reduced Irish Spring upper-arm fragrance, *Le couer* de Alain leapt up, and his abrasions of the neck were cured, and the tongue of his mouth gave praise, and far away the evil pufferfish blew and inhaled, blew and inhaled, and then forgot all about it, if indeed he ever remembered what he had done to the mighty Alain?

Up rose that boat from the ground there. That magic boat, that fairy boat. Alain got him on it and sat down real quick, because his big feet hurt and there was limited seating. He disappeared down the St. Lawrence there, and maybe he's fishing in the bayous now. And maybe wild Annie is with him, and Carl the Juggler, Francois-of-the-Canoe said to the children, not believing it, because all the heroes just died, and that was it there.

CHAPTER LXXXVII

HONEYMOON ON ALDERAAN

As I said of my recent divorce
You've got to consider the source:
I'd worry, I guess
If her parents' address
Is Rue Le Dark Side of the Force.

CHAPTER LXXXVIII

DIFFORD

IT WAS TAKING TOO long. Ray swiveled around in his rolly chair, making sure to stay on the Rubbermaid Chair Mat lest he roll off into an uncertain future. (Actually, Frank had taken care of that with an ingenious infra-red device that created an ion field around the rim of the mat so that a chair could not possibly go over the edge without a person feeling vaguely otherworldly just before, therefore making a quick ergonomic adjustment. But Ray had unplugged the USB cable and was riding the chair bareback, as it were, and the rug nubs were coming up close.) With a practiced hip move that always used to make Audrey smile, Ray banked his chair 270 degrees and turned to face Bette.

The process was taking too long. They were trying to download a desk with a sandwich in the pen drawer. The ultra-thin computer whirred away in the corner, emitting a squeak every now and then, as varnish, legs, handles, a desk calendar, and a hole the IT guy would stick the phone cable through came out of the slot. The result was beginning to look like a desk, but it wasn't looking that way fast enough for Bette.

"Can you write a script that will speed that thing up?" she cried.

"Maybe, but only if we interrupt the process and start again," Ray said. He knew that Bette was talking to hear herself talk. They both heard her say the following:

"Doesn't Amalgamated Entwife have full desk capability at non-hybrid fibre or higher?"

"Yes," Ray said wearily, thinking of Audrey's neck, "but their desks are little tatami ones with gingko underpinnings. We want *bigger*—like you said, 'Something we can hide John-John under.'"

"OK," Bette said sensibly, and stared at the office furniture assembling itself. Finally she left.

It wasn't raining anymore, but that didn't matter. Audrey was gone. It would be a while until someone else came along. There was a stain on his notebook where his coffee cup had been, but he couldn't find the coffee cup. He looked at the little brown circular mark the mug had left. Down at the bottom of the circle, like a marble rolling to seek the low point, Audrey had written: Time to go.

CHAPTER LXXXIX

SALON SELECTIVES

Perhaps if I just wash my hair
The thoughts in my head won't be there
But colorists doubt
I can ever comb out
This persistent unease and despair.

CHAPTER XC

A LETTER FROM JANOWICZ

MY EYES ARE FAILING ME, but I can still hear as well as I always could, maybe even better now that there's less sensory competition. When the letter came I made time to read it; I always have to make time because reading isn't something I can do spontaneously anymore. I have to get to the best-lit part of a well-lit room. Even then I'll have had my coffee and lunch so that I'll be motivated enough to piece it together. It isn't a chore; I love to read the newspaper and large-print books and any clipping anyone sees fit to send me. It's just labor-intensive. I like to think that, like the way my dimming vision has helped my hearing, the less time I have to read increases my appreciation of it.

The letter was tough to get through, even on that sunny Sunday afternoon. It was written longhand in spidery script across a sheet of yellow legal paper. I didn't recognize the handwriting, either, so when I got stuck my options for educated guesses were fewer. Still, it was a nice afternoon and the coming and going of the other old men I live with made the work pleasant.

I've just turned 102. I live in an upscale veterans' community just north of Tempe. It's upscale by comparison, I guess, because the places I've seen on the internet don't look half as good. Still, I'd rather be in my own house. I've developed the habit of falling down when I'm on my own, however, so I thought it would be best if I came here, where the staff leaves me alone as much as they're allowed to. It's of small consolation that my kids fought me to keep their dad at home, rather than the other way around. They're looking pretty long in the tooth themselves, so I wonder if my staying at home would make them feel better about their own futures.

I stroll through the place every day. There's a few fellas I play chess or backgammon with, and I've even been out for nine holes of golf with a couple of the administrators. There's nothing to complain about, other than a sense of loss that fades in and out. But everyone has that, and if you can still sense anything at 102, well, I'm told that I'm lucky. As my granddaughter says, *Whatever.*

So the chair was comfortable and my bursitis wasn't too bad, and I had a good fat Cuban cigar one of the orderlies bought for me in Mexicali. It was a good day, and the letter went this way:

Dear Commander,

With the passing of Frank, you're the last of us left. It is now time for you to lay claim to the package we brought back from Lyons. I'm sure you remember where it is, as it was you who buried it. I only wish that the rest of us could be there to set eyes on this treasure for the first time in over half a century. My part of the combination is Right 35. You have the other three coordinates. I only ask that you remember Charlie's great-grandson, Jared. He lives in Metterie and has leukemia. We all watched out for each other all these years, Major. Please watch out for Jared.

I know you've finally broken down and gone to live with the other old timers. Don't worry too much about it. All ten of us kept our hair and teeth into our eighties and nineties, and there were no flies on us up until the end, when the flies come regardless. You were always a hero to us,

Commander, and a hero to the country, even though the country doesn't know it. We were sorry to hear about Millie's passing—she was everybody's sweetheart but you were the one who got her, and that was only right.

Commander, it was an honor to have served under you and I know you'll do the right thing with our little French discovery. The world still needs you, and all the greatest heroes are the kind no one knows about. I'll always believe that.

Take care of yourself and do us proud, again.

Lt. Janowicz

I folded the letter and dropped it on the floor. My cigar had an ash half its size, and I tapped it off on the rug. I hadn't thought about my wife—really thought about her—in years. It seemed she'd been dead a lifetime, but it was only 30 years ago. We had such a wonderful time together all our lives, even when I was gone with the Army. She was beautiful right up until the day she died. Truly beautiful.

And remembering that was the only good news that letter brought me. Because I didn't know a Lieutenant Janowicz and I'd never been a Commander. There aren't Commanders in the Army, for Christ's sake. I had been stateside all five years in the service, and I'd never been to France. I hate the French and their stick-up-the-ass impression of themselves, with their Perma-Soft and their derision of Anglo-American culture. Fuck them. Next time someone's marching under your goddamn arch other than Pepe Le Pew why don't you call the I-talians? See what good it does you. And how come all your great pinups retire to become animal rights activists? Don't you have Medicare?

I sure do wish I knew who sent the letter. Frankly, it looked like it was mailed from beyond the grave. Either that or I'm the second to last left, unless that spineless Janowicz doesn't have the balls to get the package. That whole thing confused me, and I'm sure that everybody's better off with Frank dead and gone. There must be some foundation to help little Jared, too; I think he's better off not knowing his great-granddad got his rocks off digging holes with a bunch of brie-pounding morons. Hoo-ee!

CHAPTER XCI

THE BRISBANE SCOOPING JAWSTROKE EXPLAINED

A man who has blown off his limbs
No longer needs 20-inch rims
Nor e'er will he linger
With a lit ladyfinger
Or not use his chin when he swims.

CHAPTER XCII

THE LITTLE DRUMMER BOY'S BOXING DAY MIRACLE

HIS REAL NAME WAS Cleophas, and it had all started with a misunderstanding. He was beating a tattoo on his little ass-hide proto-bongo in the laundry room when he heard a knock on the front door. His father, the Innkeeper at the Bethlehem Pines Super 8 (Eight to celebrate the rededication of the Second Temple), rushed to answer. Business, which should have been great due to the census, had been depressingly slow. Still, there was something about the 15-year-old girl on the donkey and the sheepish look of her husband, who kept saying she was a virgin, that gave his father pause. If she's a virgin, Cleophas' dad said, then I'm the Messiah. His father didn't like the way the couple giggled at this and sent the two on their way, saying he'd rather see them sleep in a stable, what with their long hair and teen pregnancy.

His father was in a foul mood, a "firstborn-killin' mood" he would say, darkly, glaring rheumily at Cleophas. The boy tentatively played the opening to one of his dad's favorite songs, but he added too many self-conscious fills, at which point he was told to go play in traffic.

Cleophas hurried out. It was hailing, as if a warm front of hopes had met in a blustery snap of fears. Aside from the multitude of angels overhead, pecking at each other and smearing shit on billboards, there was no one around. Still, it was a bright, clear night. Polaris was extra-twinkly. Cleophas thought how, had he been born 10,000 years later, Vega would be the North Star. He smiled. *Who would name a star after a shitbox Chevy?*

There was a commotion around the corner. Cleophas crept up on a sandy knoll and peeked over. Dark Riders. Nosing around formlessly. He wished he'd had some elvish steel, but he didn't want to risk sneaking up to Old Man Barrow-Wight's place, and he didn't have time, anyway. He pressed himself lower to the ground and the Riders came closer.

Wait a minute, Cleophas thought, *where is my chilling sense of dread? Hold on a second.* He realized as one of their horses broke into a gay trot that these guys were just travelers. He stood, dusted himself off, and went to meet them in the street. There was usually a tip in it if people needed directions. "Where you headed?" he asked their leader, a short man even by Middle-eastern standards.

"We three kings of Orient are," the rider said, cryptically. The horses snorted as the four of them all looked at each other.

"Are what?" asked Cleophas.

The man paused a second, and then, as if addressing a slow child, said, "Of Orient."

Cleophas had dealt with Mongoloids before, because his family's hotel had a lot of soft furniture and a lady who came in twice a week to run a play group. He tried one more time.

"Where. Are. You. Headed?" he asked.

The second king, a little quicker on the uptake, replied, "We are following that star there, which shines so brightly."

"Good luck," Cleophas said, "Because, last time I checked, that star was in *space*."

"*Lo*!" cried the third one, urging his ass forward, "There He is!"

At this, the three kings nearly trampled young Cleophas in their haste to get to the manger behind the hotel. He ran after them, and was surprised to see all the cattle outside. It appeared that the couple had taken his father on his word and, what's more, kicked the animals out of the stable so that the hippie and his old lady could "crash" for the night. Strange, though, because the cattle were standing in an ordered semicircle before the manger, which was glowing with a warm light, and the three kings were doing their best to muscle their way in.

"What's going on?" he heard himself saying, elbowing what appeared to be a yak, "My father - "

He stopped cold. There was the couple, and in the girl's arms was a Child. Cleophas had noticed this before, and had wondered where the capitalization came from, but found that he couldn't think of anything associated with this Kid without a capital letter. "Jesus Christ," Cleophas said.

"I thought He was to be called 'Immanuel,'" the hippie said. It was clear to Cleophas that the husband didn't call the shots.

"I—" Cleophas began, but found he didn't know what to say. Anyway, he was hip-checked by one of the Chinamen.

"Check this out," the first king said, opening up a heavy mahogany coffer with brass hinges, "Gold."

Cleophas reconsidered his initial assessment of the first king, especially when the other two followed up with such crappy, useless gifts. Really, he thought, frankincense was what his mother burned when his father stunk up the bathroom and myrrh was what the prosties from Gaza got all over the sheets when they'd slink in for two-hour room rentals. Then again, they were in a barn and it was becoming more and more apparent that this gentleman was not the Baby's father. Something about the way he would talk to her and she would reply with a smirk and a "Yeah, whatever."

But the Newborn. This was a special Boy. Cleophas gazed at Him for a long time. Long enough for the three kings to head back to Shanghai, or wherever they came from, and never be heard from again. In later years Cleophas would often wonder whatever became of them and, considering they'd travelled all that distance to be at Jesus' birth, why they hadn't even bothered to send a card from time to time.

Finally, Cleophas worked up the power to speak.

"Hi," he said.

"Hi," Joseph said.

"Hi," Mary said, and then asked, "Do you know the drum break from 'Wipeout'?"

"'Deed I do," Cleophas replied, and proceeded to tear through "Wipeout," "Bron Y Aur Stomp," and "Tom Sawyer." Joseph looked pissed because, in reality, Cleophas was a lot closer to his wife's age than he was. But the reaction of the Child was priceless. Jesus just smiled, showing a mouth full of thirty-two teeth. Clearly this was the Son of God, with a set of precocious choppers like that.

Eventually Joseph warmed to the innkeeper's son, and the three non-divinities took turns swaddling the Child. Cleophas showed Mary, who in minutes looked like she'd never given birth at all, the back way to the laundry and to the machine that didn't require any quarters to run. Something told him the Boy wouldn't be needing any diaper changes, though. Everything smelled like vanilla.

Something also told him that it was now his destiny to exit gracefully from the story, which he did.

Cleophas returned to the inn, where he wordlessly picked up a mop and took care of the downstairs. His father gave him a look. The next morning he whipped up some eggs for everyone. Nothing special, but he added some chopped-up vegetables and a little bit of ham. With the smallest amount of salt, it was delicious. His father smiled at his mother, who at first flinched when he squeezed her hand, but soon realized she had nothing to worry about.

A few weeks later, his father took him out to the manger. There, approximately where he had first seen the Child, his father had rigged him up a makeshift drum kit with lambskin pulled taut over several sizes of earthenware bowls. Cleophas didn't know what to say.

Every now and then he'd get together with the night wind and the shepherd boy, but over the years the two of them began hearing increasingly fucked up things, and Cleophas would stay home, in a melancholy mood, and listen to a lot of Windham Hill and Mannheim Steamroller stuff on his headphones. He needed a break from the hopes and fears of all the years.

He couldn't forget the Boy, though, and was often sad around this time of year, depressed that fewer and fewer people seemed to get it. He wondered if he himself got it, if he wasn't himself a figment of someone's imagination. At times his possible lack of Being frustrated him, and other times he reassured himself with: Well, if I am 'Not,' then somebody else will have to wash the dishes.

That's what no one understood. All these characters had a function, and it wasn't to be picked apart for flaws, you know? Sometimes it was like telling a joke to a hostile crowd: No, I *don't* know why the horse was in the bar. It's not important. Just listen to the story.

The tape got to the end but didn't unspool the other side, as this duel-deck should have done. Piece of crap. He flipped it and "Baba O'Riley" came on. Don't go all Lot's Wife on us, Sally.

The phone rang. It was Christ. What had it been—33 years?

'Hey," He said.

"Hey," the Little Drummer Boy said, trying to sound cool. "I heard you had a little trouble in town."

"I've got Kings tickets. Are you coming or 'don't you exist'? 'Boo hoo, I'm a fictional character. Waah.'"

"Yeah," Cleophas said, "I'll be there—but how did You—?"

The Voice on the other end laughed. It was a beautiful sound. No one ever mentioned His really, just lovely speaking voice, and Ted Neeley doesn't count.

"Come on—" He said. "I'm *Jesus Fucking Christ!*"

CHAPTER XCIII

KING DIAMOND'S ON THE SOLES OF HER SHOES

While I'd love to go out on a date
I'm afraid that you've asked me too late
I'm planning to comb
The nits from my gnome
And listen to Mercyful Fate.

CHAPTER XCIV

ALL YOU DO IS THINK

ONE DOESN'T NEED VISCOSITY to be slippery, or depth. Just moisture and solidity. The presence of two, the absence of one, and the OK-ness of the fourth made Ray think about a dog wearing goggles and a scarf in a motorcycle sidecar. He was 30 and had never seen a sidecar in person. How many wheels did a motorcycle sidecar have? He wished he had a dog rather than. Oh my god, rather than...

"The ants have left the cat food," the neighborhood boy said.

Ray, relieved, sighed into his coffee cup. But warily, because every time he thought they were gone they'd come back, laying siege to the plastic cat food dispenser/obelisk in the corner. It was an injustice. He and Audrey weren't dirty people. And he hated the idea of the cats eating ants, though he knew they'd eaten spiders, birds, their own stool, each other, and several Basilica-strength frozen bags of the unsanctified Body of Christ from the archdiocese's strategic host reserve next door. The thought of the cats licking off an ant moustache after a hearty kibble meal made him uneasy. Plus, he and Audrey were paying rent for themselves and the cats, not insects. And the cats were ungrateful enough.

How many thousands of spheroid kibblim were in there, each personally licked by an ant? His mind reeled. He thought he should warn the world via The Internet, but he hated the world and the world deserved what was coming to it. But then came the neighborhood boy.

He had gently but purposefully knocked on their metal mesh door one Sunday morning. He wasn't someone they'd seen wandering the complex before. But Ray had left the inner door open and had been cursing the ants pretty loudly.

"I can help with your segmented insects," the boy said.

"You mean the ants?" Audrey said.

"It's all the same," the boy said. "Only the names have changed."

Audrey opened the door and the pale, thin boy walked in. Straight through the living area and into the attached kitchen, separated from the previous room by an abrupt end of rug. Then into the laundry area where the ants were.

"See?" the boy said. "Segmented. If your house weren't divisible by three, I wouldn't need to be here."

Ray both could and couldn't argue with that. Could because it was bullshit, couldn't because Audrey had already said that thing about "You mean the ants?" and Ray and the boy were like, *of course the fucking ants. Everything's a chore with you.*

The neighborhood boy got to work. The little duplex didn't have a lot of space, so Ray and Audrey rearranged magazines and wiped down the coffee table and freshened remote control batteries in the living area, while in the laundry room the boy scratched at a little board in his hand and quietly ululated. Soon, with his cleft-reeded oboe, the boy enticed a column of ants up from the nuggety depths of the kibble container.

Ray watched as the boy and the ants swayed together as Sunday's sunny kitchen filled with music. The neighbors even paused their squalling to hear. The cats stood there, their mouths open slightly, cocking their heads and dreaming of bicycles and plastic bags. The boy could not have been more than ten, yet he projected a gray-eyed solemnity over the room. Every living creature paid attention.

Then he changed his tune. This was a dangerous time. What if Ray, Audrey, and the cats became similarly entranced? But the boy had given them special glasses to wear. The melody coming out of the oboe was familiar: it was Bon Jovi's "Dead or Alive." As the ants listened, they began erecting a tower of themselves, one on top of the other as if each were a loaded six-string on the other's back. Finally, a trembling and thin monolith of ants stood staring at the boy, who had seen, and rocked, a million ant faces.

What day was it? What bottle was he drinking? It was the day after Passover, so it must have been Mogen David. The swaying vertical column of ants had gone airborne, disappearing through the ceiling as if searching for the final renewal of Michael York. Ray did not know where they went, and he knew, somehow, not to ask the boy, but to pay him, and nothing more.

Ray had gone to Costco the other night and had paid $1.64 for a hot dog combo with a 20. He had the change in his pocket, but turned to go up stairs to get the boy at least two crisp twenties, so as not to appear cheap, but the boy stopped him, saying that what was in Ray's pocket was enough.

"And don't you forget it," Ray said.

Then he thought: *Why do I sully this miracle with cheap jokes? Why do I condemn others and then proceed to bring my own particular brand of shame to things?*

And then: *Best not to think about it.*

"The ants have left the cat food," said the boy.

"Yeah," Ray said, bored already. "Heard you the first time."

CHAPTER XCV

VISIONS OF MY COUCH

To watch Jackson and Kerouac meet
On the set of "Soul Train" was so sweet
And where'er they were pallin'
"Good Times" or Steve Allen
They'd point and say, "Got me a Beat!"

CHAPTER XCVI

EVERYTHING'S AIRTIGHT

THIS IS THE WAY IT works. This is the way. THIS. IS. THE. WAY -

The sound came floating to Carl in that otherworldly pool/beach/ airplane way, and it took him a while to register it as a distress signal. Not only that, but Carl's airline thrombosis was also becoming a problem. How could he be an effective Sky Marshal if the seats were so small that they stopped the flow of blood to his parts? There was an air rage situation back in Coach (and why wouldn't there be?) and Carl couldn't get back there fast enough.

"This is the way it works:" the frenzied man was saying, "I pay 600 bucks for a seat that is so small I think I'm not headed for Cincinnati but a 24-piece Extra Crispy Bucket. I think, 'Hey, well at least I'll be able to see 'Spy Kids' on the way – "

"Sir, if you'll just settle down, you can see 'Spy Kids,'" the flight attendant said.

"I'm not finished," he said, "So then, I'm all excited to see 'Spy Kids,' but you tell me that I have to spend an extra five bucks for headphones which will allow me the privilege of *hearing* 'Spy Kids' with all the swears and innuendo edited out."

"'Spy Kids' didn't even have any foul language in the theatrical version, sir," the attendant said.

"Well the cunnilingus then," the man said, "And if that isn't enough, I turn to the guy next to me and he only paid $150 for his seat."

"I don't know what to tell you," a steward said. They were all standing around the man now. Up in first class, Carl was fumbling with his seatbelt, but all feeling had left his hands. He watched them flopping in his lap like fish that THE LORD had created out of his hands.

"So I don't want to pay an extra five bucks in addition to the 600 which is 450 more than the man sitting right next to me paid. I take out my own headphones, and I see that you have made the headphone jacks on the armrests of a diameter not seen in the rest of the world."

"Sir - "

"NOTHING IS OF THAT DIAMETER."

"Sir," now it was a third attendant, "are we going to have to land this plane and have you escorted out by the police?"

"Why?" the man said, calmly. "Isn't it wrong to charge different prices for commodities of the same value? Don't you think that $600 qualifies me at least to see 'Spy Kids' and an archived copy of 'The Mary Tyler Moore Show'?"

"It's really not polite to ask people how much they paid for things," the Captain said, over the loudspeaker. "To our left is Lake Huron."

Carl managed to get up, and he staggered a few seats back. He then regained his composure and made his way two sections back, through heavy curtains. The man was small, a little rumpled, and clearly out of line, if out of line meant heedless of the consequences of asking perfectly valid questions. He'd have to be taken down.

"Sir," Carl said. Now Carl was a big man. 6'4", 250. Football player in high school, retired border cop. "Sir, my name is Carl Anderson. I am not the same Carl Anderson who played Judas Iscariot in Norman Jewison's 'Jesus Christ Superstar'. As you might remember, that Carl Anderson was black. I am Filipino. Now what is it going to take for you to calm down and stop disrupting this flight?"

The man seemed to regain some of his poise. He straightened his hair, leaned forward a little, and said, "Mr. Anderson, I'm not familiar with the work of Norman Jewison, or of the other man that bears your name. I'm sure both are notable. I appreciate your offering me a means of solving my problem. Turns out I'm not really that interested in seeing 'Spy Kids', so I'd simply like a cashier's check for $450, which would compensate me for the extra money I paid for my ticket."

Carl considered this. Of course it was not up to him to grant this man a refund, as well-spoken as he had been. Still, in some other world, far away from our own, it might have been deemed a reasonable request. For example, one could bring a coupon from Safeway into Price Chopper and Price Chopper could beat that coupon price. Or a savvy consumer might price a car on the internet and walk that quote into his local Subaru dealership and make those rotten bastards dance. It could be *argued*. It wasn't an *outrageous thing* to *suggest*.

Carl looked around the cabin. Dozens of people crammed together. Some were obese, and maybe that was their fault. Some were too tall and their feet were out in the aisles. Some had unruly children. All of them muttering about not enough ports to stick things in or how it was different when their parents flew. Each of them grumbling for more cracker packets or little trinities of hard grapes. Everyone acting so put upon when their row-mate had to get up to go to the bathroom. And the cabin pressure compromised everyone's hearing, so there wasn't a conversation that didn't have an exasperated couple of "*What*?"s. Pathetic.

In fact, that's all people like this man were: Unruly Children. If this man's request were granted, would it solve anything, even temporarily? Even for the rest of this flight? No. Carl imagined a planeful of compressed crybabies, demanding seconds of Sprite, free headphones, and blankets bigger than facecloths. He imagined them overrunning First Class, sitting in First Class' rarefied chairs, drinking First Class' non-serving-size wine, fondling First Class' silverware! Carl stood at the point end of a $45 billion airline bailout, and these were the rights he was sworn to protect.

"Neither life nor this airline owes you a God-damned thing, buddy," Carl said.

"Well, I beg to dif—" the man said.

Carl withdrew his service revolver and put a bullet neatly between the man's eyes.

"Yeah!" a lady two rows over, almost fetally packed into her middle seat, hollered. "Soon we'll ALL want something!"

"Call Cincinnati," Carl said, feeling the blood pumping anew through his hero's veins, warming his untangled testicles, "and tell them to forget the paddy wagon. We'll need—" (and here he paused for effect, holding the curtain to Business Class open), "a fricking *hearse*."

CHAPTER XCVII

YOUR INCEL BROTHER IN-LAW

A lass from a flyover state
Would always orgasm too late
I told her, "Relax!
Should take three minutes, max
(Which is two minutes more than I'll wait.)"

CHAPTER XCVIII

FAIRTIME IN REASONABLE

HERE AT THE COUNTY FAIR, expectations are a cage. Farmer Dave just won the blue ribbon for Fattest Pig, but he didn't even bring a pig. The widow Becky has, for the twelfth year in a row, been awarded top honors for her raspberry preserves, but they're actually potato salad. When deciding between raspberry preserves and a couple of scoops of delicious potato salad, what would you pick? The widow Becky has been a sentimental favorite here since she raised a barn through her husband. My son and I have been coming here for several years, and he always asks me why some yokel will get a prize pumpkin ribbon if he brought a duck, or why the Miss County Fair crown is always awarded to someone who didn't show up. I tell Sam that it's all about potential.

He's a good boy, Sam is, and I get a hitch in my chest every time I remember that Jean and I almost didn't bring him into the world. We'd both been working so hard and money was tight as it had ever been, but one day I guess we made a providential mistake. Sam came along and changed our lives for the better. So here he is, nine years old, and he's asking questions that I'm fielding like an All-Star on a cool July evening.

"Why do people die, Dad?" he asks.

"Because it's their turn," I reply.

"Why do people have legs?"

"Because that's the easiest way to walk around. People didn't always have legs, but they evolved legs when there became a need for something to make it easier to get around."

"What's 'evolved'?" he asks.

"It's the change you make in order to stay alive," I say.

It isn't always this easy. Sometimes he'll ask questions—hard questions that I knew he needs an answer to, in order for him to evolve—and I don't have the answer. In those cases I tell him that I am still working on the answer to that one myself, and that when I make some headway I'll let him in on it. This satisfies Sam, and I've been able to keep my promises to him.

That's why tonight is as fun for me as it is for my son. I can finally give him the answer to something that's been troubling me. Why does the Fattest Pig award go to the guy who's pigless? What's wrong with the judges? The answer, I tell Sam, is not that the judges are wrong; it's that the judges are not giving up on Farmer Dave's potential. Sam doesn't get it at first.

"Farmer Dave didn't even bring a pig, Sam," I tell him as we grab some cotton candy and sit in the twilight, "that's why he has the most potential. It's limitless. If he brought a little squinty runty pig, he wouldn't have much of a chance, now would he?" Sam shakes his head vigorously. "But if Farmer Dave doesn't even *try*, then it's a world of opportunities for him."

"It's like Schrödinger's cat," says smart Sam. "When does a thing, which might be two things at once, decide to be definitely One Thing?"

"That's very Austrian of you," I say, not wanting to kill his spirit, "but I've got a news flash: the kinds of cats they use for experiments in radioactivity are, for our purposes, dead long before they get put in the box."

It dawns on Sam slowly, but soon I can see everything sort of tumbling into place. He is scanning his mind for certain unresolved issues in his short life and fitting them into his new philosophy. Like he's a Glad bag full of goldfish, I can see his thought process clearly. Now he knows why he didn't get onto the baseball team: he tried out. He knows why he was so disappointed when he lost the Spelling Bee: he studied so hard for it. And the fact that those institutions paid no attention to Sam's potential really shook his confidence

"So just...*give up*?" says Sam, his eyes bright with tears.

"Yes," I say, taking off his baseball cap and tousling his hair. "Give up but never let them see you do it. It's what we call a stealth capitulation."

"Who's 'We'?"

"Just the other guys in my men's group."

"Well," he says. "I'll try..."

"*Don't* try," I say. "That's the point. Don't ever, ever try."

So I make sure not to expect anything from Sam; we consider ourselves lucky to have him. Sam taught me that it's foolish to put your faith in anyone, because, in reality, things just happen, and expectations just muck it up. That's why Jean is gone. She felt it was her right to ask for some improvement, over time, some mossy growth of reliability. "No way, lady," I'd said, "I'm wearing my WYSIWYG overalls for the rest of my life." Tough to see her go, but high standards are for masochists.

That's why I love the County Fair. The sweet smell of the earth, the petting zoo, my dad over there at the barbecue pit ready with a free lunch. Mr. Lassiter just won the Strongman contest, even though he died last year. We head over to the stage and check out the program. Blue Oyster Cult is supposed to be playing later, but, you know, it's probably going to be Styx.

CHAPTER XCIX

SEPTIC MASCULINITY

If you see me erupting in boils
Don't daub me with unguents and oils
It's simply a means
To fill out my jeans
And wait for the glorious spoils.

CHAPTER C

WHAT WE KNOW ABOUT CHEYENNE

THERE WAS ONCE A MAN who maintained a small household by a northern shore. He had a long, sturdy stick to steady him as he roamed the hills by the coast. His food was the animals of the sparse forest and whatever vegetables were in season from the little garden behind his home. He never thought about whether or not he loved his life, so you could say he was happy. He had a dog that visited him daily, meeting him as part of its own wanderings, and the man missed the animal on the days it didn't arrive. Whatever else you might say about him, the man certainly appeared satisfied.

One day, the man went to town to barter some rabbit pelts for sugar, salt, and matches. He had quite a collection with him that day: there were voluminous white coats and jet-black silky ones, there were velvety calicoes and even some leathery brown pelts, taken from older jackrabbits. While the shopkeeper was assessing the man's trades, the man walked through the bustling Saturday morning in search of conversation. Approaching the post office, he saw the sheriff and the telegraph operator engaged in what appeared to be a heated argument.

"I tell you it's round, like a watermelon round," the sheriff was saying.

"It's flat as the gallows' board, Old Tommy," replied the telegraph operator.

On the other side of the street, a group of women was drawing water from the well, turning to maneuver back up the street with sloshing buckets. The man saw an opportunity to get close to the widow Becky, so he eased beside her and took one of the water pails.

"Much obliged," she said.

"Anything I can do for such a nice lady." The man found himself blushing, much to his surprise. The month before he had given a peppermint stick to the widow's son Caleb, and he saw the boy now, smiling at him from behind his mother's skirts.

"How do you do, Caleb?" the man asked, shaking the boy's hand firmly, respectfully, and without the condescension some childless adults show.

"I sure am fine, mister, and I thank you for the sweets last month."

"Well," the man said, fishing through his pockets for some trinket to give the boy, "I just might have another stick of peppermint for after your Saturday chores."

The man saw the look of delight on Caleb's face. How many times had he rode his uncle Jack's coattails to get a fireball or a handful of licorice when he was the boy's age? The widow Becky smiled at him warmly, peering up at him with dancing brown eyes. Maybe she would invite him over to supper on the pretext of teaching the boy to box or how to build a treehouse? He smiled back.

His heart thumped warmly—he liked the boy. He probably could teach him a thing or two, like how to trap a raccoon, or how to get a horse to cross deep water. But the boy was screaming. The man jumped out of his reverie. The widow Becky was now staring at him with an appalled expression, her cheeks pink with indignation.

Instead of licorice or a peppermint stick, the man had pulled from his pocket a 21-inch black reflective rubber dildo. In his sudden embarrassment he tried to stick it back in his pocket but mistakenly shoved it up the ass of the pastor's Irish Setter as both walked by. The dog reared up and mounted the pastor as if the latter were a 3-D vagina exhibit at a museum for the blind, and soon the pastor's plaintive if furtively exultant bleats brought the men of the local volunteer fire department, who in their zeal hosed down the gingham aprons of the local maids, already writhing in the dust like pungent jackhammers. The man stepped back in frank amazement and fell into the horse trough. The widow Becky was on him immediately, leading with her teeth, soon pulling every shred of his clothing away in her long-gestating want of a man. "I hear them grinding together in the barnyard," she kept moaning, her mouth filled with him. Caleb stood by the hitching post and wept until the sheriff, his face glazed with the spendings of Miss Nellie the bar wench, neatly put a bullet into each of the boy's eyeballs, then shot himself, his final seed arcing in a languid volley over the brow of Mr. Barney, the postmaster, whose fists were filled with the tender, willing flesh of the Sapphic orphanage girls.

Everybody laughed when the man got up from the horse trough, brushing himself off. He leaned over, picked his duster off the ground, and took some rock candy from the pockets. He'd bought a whole package on a whim, visiting his schoolmaster brother in Cheyenne. He looked around for Caleb. He bet the boy had never even seen rock candy. Women could trust a man who had seen the world.

CHAPTER CI

APOCALYPSE GROUCH

The Congo's the least of our hurts
Wrote Conrad of his Mistah Kurtz
In fact, it is said
That the ivory trade
Makes ernies of all of our berts.

CHAPTER CII

LIMERICKS OF LOSS AND REGRET

TINY HAIRS IN HER EARS stood, waved, and pointed like wheat in a gas station oil painting of a better-than-average Permian Basin sunset when, upon angling her cup to receive a blast of *semilla de jicaro* from the *boquilla de horchata,* Beatrice Loudglade, Ph. D., heard another customer say: "Detecting some tones of turmeric?"

She had stopped on the way to her morning class, parking her thin bicycle next to the sturdy *bicicleta con neumaticos gordos* of *(de)* Estrella, the horchata vendor *(horchatadera),* chafing at the man's use of the word "tones" while ignoring the slanty patriarchy of her own silent italicization.

"You mean because it's orange?" Estrella asked the man.

"Exactly," he, idling astride a battery-powered scooter, said. "There's something rather—"

"That's the *cinnamon,*" Estrella said, shutting him down. "It makes things *orange*. I wouldn't sneak turmeric in on anybody."

Loudglade secured her travel mug in a receptacle beneath her seat and moved on. She sometimes still believed that if people only listened to themselves talk, they'd stop saying stupid things. Well, if they were clamped somewhere and made to listen. Honest to God. Of all the things people had invented, why wasn't there some kind of instant feedback device that judged what someone was about to say a moment before they said it and issued a Thumbs Up or Thumbs Down? It could be a simple battery attached to a piece of felt, inserted in the soft palate ... Bea's doctorate was not in the *sciences*, but the *arts*.

And how was Estrella supposed to react, exactly? "An educated guess, to be sure," she could have said. Or: "Perhaps I added turmeric when I meant to add cinnamon—you see, they come in similar jars! But I assure you that turmeric's granules are more nuggety and I would have never made that mistake, as I am a fifth-generation *horchatadera movil*! It would be an insult to *mis antepasados* and they would come back to haunt and torture me as if I were I don't know Japanese all of a sudden, all bald and rickety in their *butoh* getups," Estrella-of-Bea's-mind may have said, internationally.

But Bea was a teacher—she heard stupid things all day. If not from the faculty, then from her own students. If anything, the scrawny man in his turtleneck and bike shorts had given her something to chew on for the uphill pedal ahead. And as she churned east to the reasonable mountaintop university, what the man said soon lost all its meaning in the accidental glory of *how* he had said it. The metrics of "(I'm) detecting some tones of turmeric" soon found themselves in the rhythm of her pedaling, sparking a Mittyesque reverie.

buh-BAba-buh-BAba-buh-BAba. The questing graduate student's fingers drummed across two screens, tapping references and ibids and et als, superscripting, asterisking, shoving them in, annotating the living shit out of her thesis to the point that, on one page, there were only six words of actual text—

While[12] *toiletries*[13] *aren't oft*[14] *called*[15–23] *brazen*[24], [25]

And a page of footnotes. The footnotes provided a kind of carbon offset for her program's Academic Malpractice insurance; there was less exposure to litigation if she covered her ass so thoroughly and early about not, for example, hyphenating the oft. She was pleased when, five years after successfully defending her thesis, she'd still see t-shirts around the campus with Hyphenating the Oft on them.

Loudglade had written her dissertation on limericks.

Limericks. The harmonica, strip mall psychic, and podiatrist/life coach of the poetry world. Yet they awakened something in her—the languid and tumescent middle-aged former high school lothario gone mostly to seed but not irretrievably—that had slumbered in the doughy folds of career academia.

As she pumped her way up the hill to the Interpretive Arts building, the lines poured out:

"I'm detecting some tones of turmeric,"
Said the penitent man to his cleric
"If I hadn't-a seen
These growths on my peen
I'd've notified Tevin, not Derek."

She didn't know what it meant. Was it an ecstatic vision? What kind of church was this that the confessor had such a chatty relationship with the parishioners? Who was Derek?

She recalled an old roommate, Sherman, who was a mooch. He'd appear in the corner when her friends had a dinner party. Loudly not asking for food, or drinks, or hash. When asked if he'd like some pasta or a hit or a shot, he'd say, "I won't say No," as maddeningly as you please.

Finally the man who would later marry Bea said, "Then say YES."

Bea would always say Yes to Unbidden Poetry.

So there it was. Had it come back? Had it never left? It was a powerful feeling, the raptorlike Limerick Urge. It was a drug.

She dismounted, locked her bike to the rack, and entered the building a little unsteady.

***

By 8:40 a.m., maybe half of the seats in her classroom were occupied, and some of those by bags and coats. Little boundaries. If this had been a subway car, look out: the hashtag rage would have been quick and merciless. Yet #Manspreading was one of those phenomena, like polio or quicksand, that was rarely seen in the field anymore despite its cultural touchstone status, the way a certain kind of person always adds "69" to screen names but when's the last time you saw two old friends greeting each other with a 69? Regardless, she had to admit that her college seminar had plenty of seats available.

Dr. Loudglade, Adjunct Professor of English Literature, knew that at least three people would wander in by 9:10, a trio that, even in October, hadn't committed to memory that Modes of Poetry (or PoModes) started at 8:30 and not at 9. Poking this atrocity through with bottle shards and sticking their dirty fingers in the holes, they had further decided that showing up ten minutes tardy for the *nine* o'clock class was also within reason.

With a last look at the clock and a sip of her road drink from down the hill, Professor Loudglade made a show of opening a heavy tome (it was her son's seventh-grade science textbook from twenty years ago that they'd replaced when he thought it was lost; her lesson plan itself was on a screen behind her) and began.

"Good morning," she said. "Trigger Warning."

"Noted," the class responded.

"I hope you've had a chance to spend some quality time with Philip Larkin," she said. Larkin's 1971 "This Be the Verse" was a beloved classic. It was one of those poems that tenured and adjunct professors alike clung to: short, profane, iambic, easy. It was a poem that, as her ex-husband and former thesis advisor said, "threw the body in the grave."

They fuck you up, your mum and dad...

Much of the class shuffled in their seats, making a show for each other that they may or may not be OK with this. Man handing on cowardice to man. But not Hannah Hand.

"...And I got out early as I could," the smart sophomore said. Hand who, at 24, had started college after a stint in the Coast Guard.

"Oh, that breaks my heart, Hannah!" Loudglade said. "You didn't like it?"

"No, I loved it," Hannah said, "but it just looks like something a mopey teen writes in her dream journal."

"Perhaps," the professor said, relishing this and yet aware of appearing too eager, "but there's *foreshadowing* in 1971 of the dream journals of future mopey teens and then there's actually *being* an *adult* mopey teen, like Professor Bethel or Morrissey. Do any of you know Morrissey?"

A hand went up.

"I'm kind of worried about cultural appropriation?" said Ben Bulben, harshing her buzz. Bulben was a good-looking kid, a know-it-all who, if he'd just read the assignments for meaning rather than finding fault, would be pleasant to deal with. But a claim of Cultural Appropriation needed to be handled carefully.

"How so?" the professor said, checking to see that the light on the camera at the rear of the classroom was green and that the lens was focusing and unfocusing as she moved her hands.

"Well, 'This Be the Verse'? It sounds to me like Larkin is appropriating speech patterns of People of Color, and *that's not cool!*" Bulben said. "What's the matter with 'This *Is* the Verse'? No metric rules broken."

"I'm not sure if you read to the bottom of the handout, Ben—" Loudglade said. If she could have caned students for Not Reading to the Bottom of the Handout, she would.

"—Just checking to confirm that the syllabus doesn't mention the whole page, just the poem?" Bulben interrupted, triumphant. "Yes. You write in the syllabus that we were to read 'This *Be* the Verse' for today, but it says nothing about reading whatever else is on the page?"

"Ah, I see," said Loudglade. "My mistake. The bottom of the handout goes into why Larkin chose the particular title he did."

School had only been in session for six weeks, but she already wanted Ben and most of his friends dead and, she fantasized, she would take the opportunity of their funerals to kill their parents for raising such awful, entitled people. "The title itself is a reference to a line from a Robert Louis Stevenson poem, 'Requiem,' that was written nearly a hundred years before. Stevenson's poem was an epitaph—"

"And we're supposed to know this for the test?" Bulben said.

"Yes, *Ben*," she said, drawing a chuckle from Hannah and a few others. "Knowing what an epitaph is would be good not only for the test but also for *life*. Even if it would be *difficult* for you to read your *own* epitaph. That's a clue."

"Then could you repeat that, but slower?" said Vartan "Vat" Hobbes and, as the professor repeated 'The title itself is a ref-er-ence to a line...' she watched 20 students whip out flexible keyboards or tap the words onto their typesleeves. By then, of course, four more students had arrived, and she repeated the Stevenson info like a weary hunter home from the hill.

"I apologize beforehand if what I'm about to say might hit some of you in a vulnerable area," she said, using a legally-accepted variant of "Trigger Warning" recommended by the college's Academic Malpractice firm. "I'm going to give you ten minutes to actually read the entire handout, including Larkin's 'This Be the Verse' and Stevenson's 'Requiem.' Then we can discuss it as a class. Those of you who have the privilege of being familiar with the handout are *warmly* encouraged to join me down front for a quick breakout session..."

Hannah joined her, and Phillip Linnett, and Faerie Kind, each of whom was a pleasure to have in class. Loudglade recalled her own near-decade in college, and reassured herself that this whole *Mimosenhaft* movement was no worse than any other sideshow; as frustrating as couching her language often was, she knew that Offense Seeking Behavior, as a phase of one's life just recently dropped from the *DSM*, was no more permanent or dangerous than Experimenting with Veganism, Considering a Double Major in Theatre, and Lesbian 'til Graduation.

"I'm sorry he's such a dick, retroactive-trigger-warning," said Faerie Kind.

"It's OK," Loudglade sighed. "He'll grow out of it. Trigger Warning Forever."

By 9:10 there was indeed a respectable 90 percent of her enrolled students in the room, and all had read the required text. After a stern warning from the professor, each had either sleeved or bagged various Devices of Distraction and were paying attention, participating, bright-eyed and caffeinated.

"Two questions," Bruff East said. "One. Stevenson is saying 'Dig my grave under the wide and starry sky.' Was it their tradition in England in the 1800s to dig graves at night?"

"I'm not sure," the professor replied. "Funerary practices then were similar to 'boutique' funerary services now, except now we don't have to worry about the cold earth getting in the way Trigger Warning—"

"—Trigger Warning—" the class responded.

"—back then, if you died in the winter, your body might be kept in a vault until the ground thawed enough to dig your grave. Today the people who go for 'traditional interment,' as it's called, have the benefit of Hot Shovels and nanopulverizers and stuff like that. But no, Bruff, I haven't found any reference to graves being dug at night as a matter of culture or tradition. Unless it's being done clandestinely as part of a crime. I'm willing to bet that Stevenson used 'wide and starry sky' because the stars are there whether you can see them or not, and when they are invisible during the day, the sky functions as a window through which the stars observe the earth, as our ancestors might."

"Thank you," East said. Loudglade had never met anyone named Bruff before, but he looked like a Bruff. "Did you just make that up?"

"Yes," the professor said, and the class laughed. After ascertaining that Bruff had forgotten his initial second question, she said, "Does anyone here have a relative or know of anyone who has had a traditional interment? If so, would you be willing to share that story?"

There was a physical murmur in the class. On the one hand, Prof. Loudglade was mostly off the hook if a student said something objectionable, but a case could be made that she had created an atmosphere of hostility by soliciting personal stories from her class. On the other, it was pretty much understood that the class was giving up its litigation card if it allowed a student to extemporize, for consent was strongly implied.

After 30 seconds of eye contact around the room, Loudglade closed the window by saying, "Is anyone going to sue anyone today? If not, I think Mr. Sam Louch has something to say. Sam?"

Sam Louch, one of the latecomers, was bony, blond, bespectacled. He adored Hannah, who had no idea. He stretched until bones cracked, which was his pre-public speaking ritual.

"We had an aunt who won the lottery and died about a year later," said Sam. "The first thing she did when she got the money was reserve a grave for a hundred years—"

Much of the class said: "Wow."

"—and she's been in there about three or four years now," Louch said.

"Was there a ceremony?" Professor Loudglade prodded. "If so, did you go?" She realized she could be pushing him too hard and that he might feel exposed and vulnerable, but in her judgment he seemed comfortable within the classroom milieu.

"Yeah, most of the family went, because none of us had been in a cemetery before. We went to a big one near Dallas. They had people playing the Scottish—?"

"—bagpipes—" Hannah said.

"*Bagpipes*! And then one of the guys playing the bagpipes ran the nanopulverizer and opened up the grave. The weird thing was that we got there early and about three spots away there was someone being taken *out* of their grave because either they'd missed a payment or the time was up. And when they took that person away, the same guy who'd dug him up threw on a kilt and started playing bagpipes for my aunt."

There was muted, mordant mirth. Recent legislation had allowed for graduate degrees to be removed from curriculum vitae if the student had missed as few as three student loan payments.

"What was the ceremony like?" Loudglade asked.

"It was really fun! We all got an engraved 10-teraflop coin with all my aunt's favorite music and art and videos on it and a commemorative case with room for nine more coins, and a player."

"Were the rights cleared?" Bruff asked.

"Yes," Sam replied. "Expensive! Not only that, but there were licenses for five distributions."

"Whoa," Bruff said.

"Can you use the player for other flopcoins?" Hannah asked.

"Yeah, it's a multi-use player, but it's a really nice one. It's *heavy*." Louch made complementary Ls with his hands and held them about a foot apart to show the size. "You can plug all kinds of old media in there. But the bagpiper was really trying to sell my father and his brothers on getting buried there, too, because the player fits a bunch more coins, he was saying."

"A lot of cemeteries in the west have these leisure and media communities around them," the professor said. "Are you likely to visit again?"

"Yes, there's a nice fitness center there, and you can unlock my aunt's hologram with the coin. She could have actually recorded up to a day's worth of video, different speeches and whatnot, but she chose to record ten separate minutes, so each time we're there we'll hear a different thing. It's *NICE*."

"*NICE*," the class agreed, echoing the falsetto.

"I've never been to a cemetery myself," Loudglade said. "But I read that some of the big American ones are making a push to gameify. It must help keep your aunt's memory alive, no? To be able to unlock new messages with each visit? Do you feel closer to her, knowing that you're standing on the ground she's buried in?"

Some of the class expressed uneasiness with this, a low, open-mouthed vibration, and the professor wondered if that would show up in today's critiques. She didn't want to hit her semester's Dismissable Negatives ceiling, because she'd already spiked close to the threshold several days into the class when she gently chastised some of the tardies.

"Well, the coin lets us into the franchise cemeteries and we can call her up from any of them. I did that when I did Outward Bound in the Marshall Islands, and they had a branch over there. They've got a room where you deposit the coin and a pretty good approximation of the home cemetery comes up. But it wasn't the same as the place where she's actually renting some earth (the class: "*Ohh.*") I can't see going to a different cemetery just to scroll through her messages. I'd like to go to the actual one and stand there, you know? It feels more real."

"*NICE.*"

"Plus we found a lot of good food trucks around there. I guess it's part of the cultural profile around Dallas to go to food trucks after a funeral."

"I didn't know that. Thank you for sharing!"

This was a good, guided discussion. Professor Loudglade had a certain amount of defensible wiggle room to follow a conversation outside of the lesson plan, and she felt this morning's discursion from Philip Larkin to epitaphs to funerary customs to personal revelations would hold up to any review. Still, that was always the landmine in the Interpretive Arts—an instructor could be tried up to three years after the class ended in case a grain of nanoaggression became a litigable pearl in the mouth of the Clam of Indignation. She sometimes wished she taught maths, but even those classes could get ugly when thoughtless professors placed parentheses provocatively.

Loudglade ended the class by reading Larkin's "Posterity," his poem written in the style of an imagined biographer. "After he died, a lot of his letters and early works were published, and they didn't reflect well on him. It revives the ancient and enduring dilemma of separating the art from the artist. So, if you don't want to be referred to as 'One of those old-type natural fouled-up guys,' *or ladies*, when your mopey teen poetry is published posthumously," she said, "never write anything down, ever."

Bea looked at her notes, crammed in neat, wavy lines complementing the lacunae of Larkin's "High Windows," a sturdy paperback she found at a Santa Fe estate sale for 15 bucks. Then, for the first time, she noticed some lines in Anthony's tight script. They would appear later in his collection "Beatrice in Purgatory."

You won't be thanked; You'll be dismissed
Your work a slap upon the wrist
The ones with whom you did your time
Will all survive you in a rhyme
They, turning from your webby grave
Will but lament the fucks they gave.

The professor paused. In a moment, her eyes had taken in more information than they were used to. Where had she been when Anthony, her ex, her mentor, the father of their child, had borrowed her book and doodled in it?

"So please send in your essays by Friday," she said, not looking at them, "or I will *fail you*."

She biked home, past the gated mansions of Albuquerque's Brinksman billionaires, to the second floor of a triple decker she shared with two fellow college employees—one was a tenured professor and the other was the dining hall manager, who owned the building.

"Bea," said Jane Bishop, sprawled on a ratty couch with her cat, Ratty, "I'm here to answer any questions about the package on your bed."

"Thanks, Jane," said Beatrice, feeling a tinge of remorse that she had, just a few nights before, perhaps shared too much personal information with her older, more evil colleague. She lingered outside her bedroom, shifting her gaze between the cardboard box and her lounging roommate, wanting to tear open the package in privacy but not keen on being asked to narrate its contents. "So—."

"I'll let you go," Jane said, thumbing the nub of a device and staring at it over the triangle head of Ratty. "We'll catch up at dinner."

Thus dismissed, Beatrice closed the door both as securely and as quietly as she could, jammed a promotional ballpoint pen from a plagiarism-detection subscription service into the top of the box, tore the lid asunder, and emptied her bounty onto the quilt.

Tumbling out came what looked like an avalanche of children's blocks—let's call them Legos—alternately containing a Master's thesis, several attempts at novels, screenplays, the documentation from an undergraduate archaeological dig, or terabytes of unsorted photos and videos and audios. The box itself brought a smell of decayed paper to her neat little room, recalling pleasant trips to local libraries back in Mississippi. The databricks, too, were relics, as she'd inherited a box of them from her father, wiped them when he upgraded to—what? She couldn't remember—and employed them all the way through high school, college, and postgrad, until no reputable organization used, accepted, or played them anymore. Until generations of devices had long since abandoned port space for them. And when she and Anthony divorced, she'd left much of her life in that little box at the back of his small garage.

At the time it was satisfying to dump the fifty or so primary-colored bricks into the box and seal it up before she moved, a small, deceptively heavy box. She felt like she was putting away childish things. (Then her mother arrived with the U-Haul and destroyed the mood.)

It had been years since she'd even seen a databrick. They were dense ("Dense with Data" was how Mavervorl Labs sold them), like smooth-edged rectangular rocks. Several semesters ago some native artisans had strung a few together and were selling necklaces of bricks and turquoise at the student union during Orientation. Her freshmen looked like sacred fools until maybe the second week of September.

And here was her past. A past before her son, straddling her own young adulthood and the few years of her early marriage that weren't muddled by her husband's work or her own resentment. She had a player on her dresser that looked like a model of a double-wide trailer. You could get players that resembled dollhouses, warehouses, cars, submarines, tract homes, mansions, filling stations, etc. She liked the double-wide design with its lifelike-enough garden and its brickport that doubled as the trailer's front stoop. So even though it had been a decade or more since she'd used a databrick, the players themselves were often so sturdy and arty that people displayed them like they would ancient, well-framed yard sale photographs of the unrelated deceased.

She found the brick she was looking for—the lone green one (not to be confused with the *Lorne* Greene one, a specialty item that only fit players that looked like the Battlestar *Galactica*). She plugged it in, clicked Connect on her typesleeve, and faced the blank wall. The following appeared, and Beatrice burped a gasp at the out-of-favor font. She'd forgotten about it.

Themes of Regret in 21st Century Limericks
Beatrice Loudglade, MPhT Candidate, 2029

Derided as, at best, a delivery system for nonsense or, more commonly, obscenity, the limerick has been overlooked in its capacity to express beauty, sorrow, and political thought in its brief five lines, much like the haiku is no longer associated with flatulence, which was its exclusive use in feudal Japan.

This paper traces the limerick's history and proposes the form's renewed and expanded usefulness for lovers of the sciences, food preparation and, of course, great literature.

Built into this verse from 1946, however, we can see the dismissive tone many critics took with the limerick:

Your poems are base and domestic?
Try meter that's not anapestic
If a chick named Aqaba
Joins the Swedes in ABABA
Then "Fernando" gets way more majestic

Yet even as the writer's scorn drips from the page, the limerick comments not only on the then-recent sovereignty of Transjordan but also foreshadows by nearly three decades the establishment of the preeminent Swedish supergroup/acronym. Perhaps the limerick's usefulness is so easily discounted because its power is so awesome.

Shuddering in the wave of juvenilia, she turned from the impromptu wall display, rippling but easily readable over the uneven surfaces of picture frames, bookcase, and sad houseplants, and faced the little double-wide player, feeling the heat from the beam on her sternum. There was no note from Anthony. Even the addresses on the box were generated labels. Was the lack of a note itself a note, a gentle acknowledgment that he no longer cared?

There was a park by the Rio Grande that occasionally offered a view of a muddy, flowing river. Today she had no such luck as she ditched her bike on a tree stump and gazed at the swaying weeds in the wash. She remembered firing off messages to Anthony until her left arm felt like it wasn't attached to her anymore. And where were those messages now? Data-mined, encrypted and recrypted, keywords lifted blind and out of context from her private correspondence to be geo-tracked, sold, and targeted back at her. She knew this—every user of a free storage service knew this—so she and Anthony would occasionally invent words, like "burmula" or "enterpations" (the bones atop one's shoulders and the dimples above one's buttocks, respectively), just to see where those neologisms would pop up three months later in some serialized commercial or coupon.

And as she sat by the river, all she could think about was how charming and essential that digital repartee seemed at the time. She remembered nothing but the feeling of needing to see what came next, if it was an affirmation or a setback. But, even if compelled by a judge, she would not be able to call up any of the words she and the father of her child had exchanged 30 years ago. There was no box of decaying letters—it was all ones and zeroes transmitted over a series of proprietary devices that didn't really talk to one another using services that flew by night, went out of business, and more often than not sold and sent all their compiled data to an orbiting belt of bytes. Were there aliens, all that discarded binary space trash had surely sterilized them by now.

If, along with everything else, Anthony's obituary had fluttered out of that box onto her bedspread, Bea would have felt relief. Instead, her regret came in the loss of the words they'd sent each other when they were in love. She knew, but more academically than any other way, that those words had once meant the world to her. Surely there was somewhere else they existed now, in some redundant array, but they'd lost whatever gave them force. Dead weight words, barely a gigabyte of them.

She remembered these words from the convocation of Vatican III:

I'm sure that your mother is proud
That you keep all your shit in the Cloud
But Our dear Lord encouraged
More tangible storage
Which is why His beak's smeared on a shroud.

Across the river was a hulk of a building. In its century it had been a hospital, a university extension, lofts, and a light assembly factory. Its latest incarnation found it warehousing data, and in this endeavor it had flourished. Buildings had been added and cellars had been dug. It extended a quarter mile across and who knew how far down. Places like this dotted the Southwest and were basically the lifeblood of the former No Man's Land between Ensenada and Cabo San Lucas, too. They were mausoleums of ancient data stored on all manner of drives and devices, constantly powered up and searchable thanks to a family's low monthly subscription fee. Then, once the last loved one passed (the data warehouses could wait), pictures, dream journals, videos, spreadsheets, voice recordings, and every keystroked footprint that comprised a human life was available for purchase. Bea remembered seeing an erectile dysfunction medication commercial as a girl that featured her beloved grandfather, just five years dead. She shouted to her mother and the two of them watched the screen as the series of animated photos and audio snippets combined to show Grandpa Eddie gravely lamenting the loss of his boner.

"Now I can go into my russet years confident," Eddie intoned. "Thanks for straightening me out, Turgidor."

"Ugh," her mother had said. "I didn't renew that debit card."

The drone bay at the supermarket was a humming hive this afternoon. On her way here from the river, on the footbridge by Rio Bravo, Bea had stopped her bike to watch an ease of drones heading upriver. Some of them, she bet, were here now. The drone bay smelled like ozone and was peaceful and blue in low light. It was a building tacked onto the supermarket, occupying what had once been the parking lot. Now Bea anchored her bike and walked into "historic" Keltons, smiling at a few university colleagues and students who were similarly engaging in in-person-shopping-as-anthropology. There was sawdust on the floor despite the place being smell-free, humidity-free, almost human-free.

She picked up a bag of onions, some steaks, a bottle of Pueblita (a locally-sourced high-ion cooking odor neutralizer for Janet's benefit), oranges, butter, and a braid of garlic, then headed for the liquor aisle.

And, just as she had when she was a student herself, Bea would get a couple of bottles of wine in person, mark the rest of her groceries for delivery, and race the drones home. However toned she got—and Bea was fitter now than she was at 20—she had never beaten one.

On her way out of the liquor aisle, she spotted a bottle of Sullen Times and stopped. New plan. She watched her right hand curling around the familiar polyhedral neck, languidly placing the rotgut in her basket. It was the whiskey that sealed the deal with Anthony and it tasted like—a tire store? Loss? Turmeric? She'd pour some into her travel mug, bike down Las Lomas, sit on the shallow steps of Zimmerman Library on the University of New Mexico campus, and knock it back. Then she'd give the rest of the bottle to a student. After all, UNM wasn't her school anymore.

But before that, a ritual: Completing her purchase required the standard thumbprint, but since Kelton's still had the scanners that customers could take to the very door, just in case there was an impulse buy of a candy bar or a gourd on the way out, many people, including Bea, would back up to the door with their items in one hand and the portable thumbprint scanner in the other. Thumbing the screen instantly transferred cash and summoned the drone, so it was like a starting gun. Bea backed to the door, thumbed the scanner, heard it beep, and opened her hand as the device whizzed back to the checkout line.

And that's when she turned to see her ex-husband Anthony, his new wife Liesl, their own four-year-old with a stupid name, and Bea's and Anthony's son, David. David, whom she hadn't seen in six years, looked just like his father. The family walked right by her, very likely didn't see her. She gripped the neck of the Sullen Times bottle, feeling like she could snap it if she tried hard enough. She walked to her bike as her grocery drone emerged from the bay. She pushed off and pedaled with thigh-burning gusto down the road.

People in some parts of the country occasionally fired on the drones, and any time a new market sprouted up in some benighted area, certain locals would react atavistically, seeing in the drones some threat or challenge. But this behavior died down quickly, as companies learned that all they needed to do was temporarily ground all their drones when one got shot at, trapped, or otherwise molested. That brought the weight of Popular Consumer Indignation down on the saboteur, who was nearly always debited an exorbitantly punitive amount. Now the drones lived in smug coexistence with yokel and pillar alike, and even when one occasionally decapitated some statistically irrelevant for our purposes slob en route to delivering a jar of cashews, society absorbed the tragedy as the offset of convenience. Herself, Bea usually found their hums and muted lights soothing.

But not tonight. "I look like a wizened old crone," she repeated every time her pedals reached twelve and six. "I look like a wizened old crone." She felt the machine gaining on her, saw a dim blue light on the road ahead as it signalled its course, and she wondered when it would decide that its route was optimal and hers was inelegant. At times like this, when she'd feel her road and the drone's diverging, she'd occasionally feel sad, like it had a wisdom she didn't.

But she turned right, and so did the drone. She thought, "It likes me." She thought:

Let's say I had sex with a drone
I was lonely; it followed me home
And though I've a penchant
For beings more sentient
It was way more engorged than my phone.

And maybe she was in better shape after all. She'd sunk into a rhythm with the limerick, and the hum had grown faint and the light dim. She was pumping so hard, she felt like a dog on a long lead, pulling its master, whose blue eyes shone farther and farther back, farther up.

At home was her tidy room. Home *was* her tidy room. In her tidy room was the little piece of art she was working on, in which she'd crush databricks into a mosaic, then crush the mosaic and glue its parts onto a series of microchips. She'd spend some cash on some eighth-party launch-for-hire outfit out of Durban or Wherever to send the chip into space, where it could be bombarded with lasers and super-cooled to a hair north of absolute zero. For six minutes or so, until the fragile Bose-Einstein condensate broke apart, her life in digital form, comprised in jangly atoms of rubidium, lithium, and multicolored plastic, would be a fifth state of matter, in space, and then nothing. And she could stream it. The very ephemerality of the project, and its just-as-quickly-forgotten artist statement accompanying it, would probably get her tenure. The idea had just occurred to her in a burst of carbon dioxide.

She crested a rise and the drone, newly confident, overtook her, sailing toward the Sandia foothills. She wouldn't catch it. But the momentary sadness didn't come; instead a strong, fleeting urge to huck the bottle of Sullen Times at it and sabotage both evening and bank account did. She didn't act on it.

She coasted to the library, her legs like twin beanbags, and was good for maybe two brazen swigs from the bottle before she realized this scene wasn't for her. And she felt self-conscious, all of a sudden, about staggering out of the darkness to gift a used bottle of whiskey to a teen. How would this look? Would she say she had been to a bachelorette party? A book club? And there was this, you know, extra half-consumed bottle of shitty alcohol?

"*Profesora*?" came a familiar voice by the street. It was Estrella on her fat-tired horchatacycle. Bea waved with her bottle hand and ambled toward her. "Looks like you're off duty."

"Yup," Bea said.

"You have a look about you that makes me think you were about to throw that bottle away," Estrella said.

"I was going to give it to someone," Bea said.

“A student?”

“Yep.”

“Pour that in the horchata, it’s an excellent drink,” Estrella said. “It’s like Christmas.”

“OK.”

Estrella produced two liter travel cups and, with her thumb on the nozzle of (what Bea now realized was) the homemade horchata receptacle/dispenser contraption, directed twin sprays into the cups, which she balanced on her thigh, raised like the leg of a horse statue. She then grabbed the bottle of whiskey from Bea and poured two generous dollops into their drinks. She handed Bea her cup and kept the bottle.

They toasted and sat side by side on the curb, watching the students, the occasional drone, the last of the sunset, and the first of the bats.

“This is delicious,” Bea said.

“And no fucking *turmeric*,” Estrella said.

“Ha! ‘Detecting some tones—’”

Bea thought about telling Estrella that she’d crafted a limerick from that morning’s exchange, but then thought she’d have to explain what a limerick was and then explain the gay Catholic subtext, not to mention explain why any of it mattered. Was she demeaning Estrella by not thinking her up to the conversation, or was she worried that Estrella wouldn’t even care? It didn’t seem enough that Bea’s audience of herself was gleeful about those five lines.

"I'm not much of a poet," Bea said, in the end, to no one, really.

"Well I'm not even Mexican," Estrella said.

CHAPTER CIII

AT THE MINASMORGULMAT LAVANDERIA

"The machine nearly ruined my pleats,"
Cried the Witch King whilst folding our sheets.
"But I thought I'd take weeks
Washing out all the streaks
From when I fed Horsey fell meats."

CHAPTER CIV

UMBERELLA

YOU ARE RIHANNA, AND you are preparing to sing "Umbrella" to me. It is a song of devotion and eternal friendship. Though it was written by other gentlemen and rejected by the handlers of Britney Spears and Mary J. Blige before you agreed to do it, it is your song. It is a song in which you assert, timidly, that in darkness, all trappings of material wealth are stripped away. The umbrella, you feel, is a symbol of the sheltering nature of our relationship. So adamant are you that I understand this that you add an extra syllable to the word, pronouncing it "Umberella." I don't correct you, because Alexander Hamilton also came from the West Indies.

But just as you are getting into your outfit to sing the song to me, there is a knock on the door of our breezy cabana. It is your producer, Jay-Z. We remain unsure if he had been listening just outside.

"Uh Huh. Yeah," he says. "I've got a little rap I'd like to do to introduce the song."

"To introduce the song on Merv Griffin?" Rihanna asks.

"No, Hoo!" Jay-Z replies. "I'll do a little rap at the beginning of the song. On the record. And when I'm done with my little rap, you sing the song."

"But why do I need an introduction on the song?" Rihanna says. "Was there an introduction on 'Stairway To Heaven'? Or 'Mama,' by Phil Collins-era Genesis?"

"Check it," Jay-Z says, unfolding a bar napkin. "I wrote my rhymes here. Listen:

Uh-huh, uh-huh. Yeah, Rihanna
Uh-huh, uh-huh. Good Girl Gone Bad!
Uh-huh, uh-huh. Take three, action.
Uh-huh, uh-huh. Hov.
No clouds in my stones
Let it rain, I hydroplane in the bank
Coming down like the Dow Jones
When the clouds come, we gone, we Roc-A-Fella
We fly higher than weather, in G5's or better
You know me (You know me)
In anticipation for precipitation, stack chips for the rainy day
Jay—Rain Man is back
With Little Miss Sunshine, Rihanna, where you at?

And then you sing the song."

(The three of us sit in silence for a moment.)

"Like, right after you ask where I'm at, I immediately start the song?" asks Rihanna. "In the world of your little rap, have I snuck up behind you?"

"Naw, see, hoo," says Jay-Z.

"My song is about my devotion to a friend that I happen to be attracted to," Rihanna says. "Your little rap is about cash, and the bank, and how you have a plane that may be better than a G-5."

"Uh huh," Jay-Z says. "Yeah."

"And there's a line in my song about how, in the dark, no one sees shiny cars. It is a song that eschews materialism."

"Hoo!" Jay-Z says.

"I mean, this little rap intro is all about you, is both irrelevant to and contradicts the song I'm about to sing, and in fact subtracts from the song, massively," Rihanna says.

"Hova, please understand," I say, taking him aside. "I like what you do, but did you know that, in the 30s and 40s, when the tap dance break came around in songs, people hated that, too? It's like, 'Somebody was singing a moment ago, and it was fine, and now I have to listen to their *feet*?' You remember how in Salt-n-Pepa's 'Push It' there was suddenly a rap on one of the remixes?"

"'Push It' was a dope song," Jay-Z says. "I don't know why that man started rapping in the middle of it. It was jarring. But what *I'm* doing is at the *beginning*."

"It doesn't matter," I say. "Everything you wrote on this napkin is self-serving and ridiculous. It seems like you are hijacking Rihanna's song."

"Hoo! Uh huh," Jay-Z says.

"If it makes you feel any better," I reassure Jay-Z, "your gratuitous and embarrassing little rap is the pinnacle of a trend that will only devolve to Juicy J's introduction to Katy Perry's 2013 'Dark Horse.' Listen:

Oh, no
Yeah
Ya'll know what it is
Katy Perry
Juicy J, aha
Let's rage

"He says 'Oh No' and then 'Yeah' like something suddenly changed," says Jay-Z, studying his napkin.

"In a bit of dramatic irony, 'Dark Horse' was successfully challenged for copyright infringement."

"Why was that dramatic irony?" Jay-Z asks.

"Because Dark Horse was also George Harrison's record label, and he also got charged with copyright infringement for 'My Sweet Lord,' and you call yourself J-Hova."

"Who's George Harrison?"

Rihanna has changed into a light sweater and slacks.

"What we're saying is that if your little rap isn't some nakedly patriarchal ploy to pee on the tree of my song, then at best, people are going to like the song *despite* its opening," Rihanna says. "And that is true of all rap intros and rap breaks in every song that is not itself a rap song, ever."

"What about Blondie's 'Rapture'?" Jay-Z asks.

"That was a terrible rap song, as was Sugar Hill Gang's 'Rapper's Delight.' We are lucky the art form survived them."

"And you know that 'Umbrella' is an awesome song without your little rap in it, right?" I say. "And that people who otherwise like your little raps enjoy the songs comprised totally of them, right?"

"Uh huh. Hoo."

"And even with 'Empire State of Mind,' Alicia Keys was adding a musical break to your rap song, and not the other way around. Do you understand?" Rihanna asks.

"I promise I will never add my little raps to anyone else's songs again," Jay-Z says. He crumples the napkin, but does not toss it into the wicker basket Rihanna offers to him. Instead, he shoves it into his pocket and leaves wordlessly.

"You should go," Rihanna says. "Something inside tells me that we have finished our journey together. I'll always remember you for saving my single, 'Umbrella,' and allowing it to be uncompromised. Know that I'll always be your friend."

As I leave, I pass Jay-Z practicing the rap in the courtyard. He seems so earnest and intense, addressing his rhymes to an assemblage of likely fronds. Of course his rap was stapled onto "Umbrella" and, just like Juicy J's ridiculous "Let's rage!" preceded Katy Perry's "Dark Horse," losing Hillary Clinton the 2016 election, those kinds of high-level hip hop hijinks are what the "Lemonade" album is about.

CHAPTER CV

MY AUDITION FOR "8 MILE"

The neighbors are out dropping dimes
On my lute-shredding limerick crimes
They're shrieking, "J'accuse!
Where's our tasteful haikus?"
While I'm up in this tree spoutin' rhymes

When this kaiju slinks outta the river
The pillars of town start to shiver
My sick metric beats
Have 'em hosing their sheets
As I spit fire of 'gnac from my liver

White wine-swilling fools get annoyed
When my odes leave their buildings destroyed
But my sweet words, so freighted
Leave whole towns impregnated
Like a load-bearing protocol droid

Even the coarsest of chimp'll
Cinch up his stiff Puritan wimple
Crying, "What hath God wrought?"

'Gainst the verbal onslaught
Of lyrical pus from brain pimple

So crawl thou straight under the earth
If you quail at this glorious birth
O, you'll drown in the gush
From my foot-florid flush
And my surfeit'will be your sad dearth!

(Drops mic through continental shelf)

Born in Lowell, Massachusetts, Marty Barrett now lives near the Lowell exit of the 210 freeway in Los Angeles. He thinks "The Lowell Exit" would make a good signature cocktail or euphemism for suicide, but only plans to try one, depending on the ingredients.

Fogelfoot Press

Who knows if the internet will even exist by the time this slab of traditional media comes out, but reliable sources of information about Mr. Barrett, the rock opera "All That Jaws," Fogelfoot the band (which has set a few of the stories in this book to glorious music), and other Fogelfoot-adjacent events remain martybarrett.com and fogelfootpress.com.

www.ingramcontent.com/pod-product-compliance
Lightning Source LLC
Chambersburg PA
CBHW060628310726
48982CB00003B/712